the Death of Bees

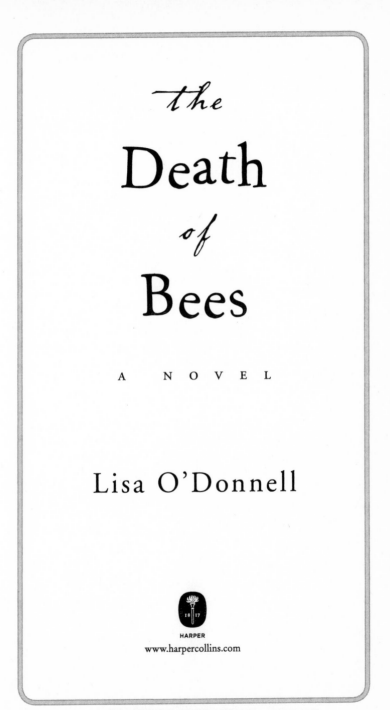

the

Death

of

Bees

A   NOVEL

Lisa O'Donnell

HARPER

www.harpercollins.com

THE DEATH OF BEES. Copyright © 2013 by Lisa O'Donnell. All rights reserved. Printed in the United States of America. No part of this book may be used or reproduced in any manner whatsoever without written permission except in the case of brief quotations embodied in critical articles and reviews. For information, address HarperCollins Publishers, 10 East 53rd Street, New York, NY 10022.

HarperCollins books may be purchased for educational, business, or sales promotional use. For information, please e-mail the Special Markets Department at SPsales@harpercollins.com.

Originally published in Great Britain in 2012 by William Heinemann, an imprint of the Random House Group.

FIRST U.S. EDITION

Designed by Michael Correy

Library of Congress Cataloging-in-Publication Data has been applied for.

ISBN 978-0-06-220984-9

13 14 15 16 17   OV/RRD   10 9 8 7 6 5 4 3 2 1

To my children, Max and Christie

the Death of Bees

Prologue

Eugene Doyle. Born 19 June 1972. Died 17 December 2010, aged thirty-eight.

Isabel Ann Macdonald. Born 24 May 1974. Died 18 December 2010, aged thirty-six.

Today is Christmas Eve. Today is my birthday. Today I am fifteen. Today I buried my parents in the backyard.

Neither of them were beloved.

Winter

Marnie

Izzy called me Marnie after her mother. She's dead now, actually they're both dead. I'm just saying that's how I got it, my name. My mum had a boring name, didn't suit her at all. She was an Isabel called Izzy. She should have been a Charlie, I think of her as a Charlie. My dad had a gay name, Eugene. He never said he hated it, but I bet he did. Everyone called him Gene, but he was a bit of a Frankie, a Tommy, maybe a Mickey. My pal Kimberly gets called Kimbo, she's always getting into fights and would smack her own shadow if she thought she could catch it. Kimbo's name evolved from a slagging she got for being a total psycho and it stuck, like a warning. "Here comes Kimbo, run for your life."

My other pal is Susie. Her real name's Suzanne and for a long time that's what we called her, we never felt inclined to shorten it the way people do with long names, but then when we were about eleven years old she told us she didn't want to be called Suzanne anymore, she wanted to be called Susie. She thought it sounded older and sexier, I suppose it does. Of course her granny still calls her Snoozy, mortifying baby name.

Then there's my sister, Helen, we call her Nelly, to be honest I don't think she knows her name is Helen, she's been Nelly since she was a baby. Nell would have been cooler, but she was like Dumbo when she was born, so Nelly was a perfect fit.

Izzy said choosing my name was a nightmare; she wanted something different for me, something sophisticated that made people look twice at me, as if they'd missed something about me the first time they looked, and so she chose her mother's name. I understand Emma was also a hot favorite, so was Martha, but Gene didn't like Emma, he said it was a weak name. He didn't like Sam either because he got dumped by a Sam. He also knew a Siobhan who got smacked by a bus when she bent down to pick up a fag end on the curb side. Gene's favorite was Elise because of a song by the Cure, but Izzy hated it, she was more of a New Order fan and I understand Elegia was discussed.

Izzy said I was tiny when I was born, a preemie rushed to the intensive care unit where I was kept in a plastic bubble for nine weeks with Gene and Izzy peering at me through Perspex glass. The safest place I've ever been. Anyway that's why I'm Marnie and not Eve or Prudence or Lucretia. I'm Marnie. Too young to smoke, too young to drink, too young to fuck, but who would have stopped me?

People think Nelly's nicer than me, but only 'cause she's off her head. She's twelve. She likes cornflakes with Coke and period dramas. She likes old movies with Bette Davis and Vivien Leigh. She likes documentaries about animals and anything to do with Harry Potter, she's obsessed with him. She also plays the violin courtesy of Sarah May Pollock, a music teacher who weeded out talent every year by forcing us to listen to recorded notes. I was never selected to play an instrument, although I like to sing and can hold a tune pretty well, but it was Nelly who identified the treble clef necessary to play the piano, an instrument she boked at, drawn instead to a lone violin with a broken string lying flat on a gray Formica table. Obviously she plays brilliantly and within a short period of time Miss Pollock ended up giving her the violin for keeps, a gift last Christmas, that's how good Nelly is or how good Miss Pollock was who loved to play with her. Unfortunately Miss Pollock left the school, was replaced by Mr. Charker, a trumpet man. Nelly still plays and like a master someone said and of course our school gives her a platform every Christmas mostly to wow the board of governors even though the school is not advancing her in any way by hiring someone else to teach her. Not that it would make any difference when she can actually play without music. Kimbo and Susie love to hear her play, so do the neighbors and I like it too except when she pulls it out in the middle of nowhere and starts in with the Bach because she does that, on the subway sometimes, in a bookstore on Sauchiehall Street, and on a bus to Wemyss Bay once. No one ever minds, 'cause she's so good but it sort of embarrasses me, her zipping away and me next to her smoking a fag like a total stranger, as if we don't belong together.

Another little foible of Nelly's is how she talks. She sounds like the queen of England most of the time. She doesn't say *mum*, she says *mother* and she doesn't say *dad*, she says *father*. She has sentences in her head like "What the devil's going on?" and "What on earth's all this hullabaloo?" I've also heard her say "confounded" and "good golly." Drives me nuts. Constantly having to protect her from head cases who think she's taking the piss. She also wears spectacles, round ones like Harry Potter; she's recently developed an obsession with him and wears them like they're real glasses, except they're not. Last Christmas Izzy got her a magic cloak, but she only wears it around the house and one time to take out the rubbish.

Truth is Nelly's a wee bit touched, not retarded or anything, just different. She doesn't have many friends, she doesn't laugh much, and when you talk to her about something serious she gets really quiet, like she's taking it in and then rearranging it in her head. I don't know how she arranges it, I just know it's different from how I might arrange it. She also takes things very literally, so you have to be careful what you say. For instance if I said, "You're fucking mental," she'd say something like, "I can assure you, Marnie, one is perfectly sane!" I don't know why she's not dead to be honest. You can't talk like that, not in Maryhill.

Gets to you after a while, even the teachers, they can't deal with her at all. When she started secondary school they put her in a class for total fannies, but halfway through the school year they had to take her out 'cause she's totally brainy at science. Pure Einstein stuff and then of course there's the violin. I feel sorry for her. I mean she can't help it, being how she is, it's not like she wants to say everything in her head. She can't help it, like telling the toughest girl in her year, Sharon Henry, she should wash her "down theres" 'cause Nelly could smell her "foulness." Seriously. No censor. Lucky for her Shaz thought it was funny, which meant everyone else was permitted to say it was funny, even luckier, it wasn't said in front of any guys. Apparently Shaz grabbed a bar of soap and told everyone she was off to wash her "down theres" and then simulated cleaning aforementioned unmentionables. Hysterical laughter ensued interrupted by an irate Miss Moray, who wants everyone to fuck off so she can have her lunch. Now whenever any of the girls from Nelly's class walk past her they simulate washing their vaginas or ask her if she can smell fanny. Nelly doesn't get it. Tells them not to worry—"They're perfectly sanitary."

There's other stuff of course, like the rabid chitchat and usually about something totally random. I remember when Steve Irwin died, the reptile guy, for about a month it was the only thing she'd talk about. Steve Irwin's widow, his daughter, and of course stingrays. Where stingrays live. What stingrays look like. How to get poisoned by a stingray. You want to thump her when she gets like that.

I prefer the Harry obsession, it's quieter. When Nelly's reading, nothing exists, not even me, I love it when she's reading, I like not existing, even for an hour. I think the Harry Potter thing reminds her of Nana Lou. She read a couple of the books to her when she took care of us that time but those days are well over. We're on our own now. Izzy and Gene are dead and no one can know what we've done with them. We'd get separated for sure, they'd put me in a home and God knows what they'd do to Nelly. Anyway I'll be sixteen in a year. They can't touch me then. I could have a baby at sixteen and get married, I'm considered an adult and legally able to take care of both of us.

I suppose I've always taken care of us really. I was changing nappies at five years old and shopping at seven, cleaning and doing laundry as soon as I knew my way to the launderette and pushing Nelly about in her wee buggy when I was six. They used to call me wee Maw around the towers, that's how useless Gene and Izzy were. They just never showed up for anything and it was always left to me and left to Nelly when she got old enough. They were never there for us, they were absent, at least now we know where they are.

Nelly

G ood God, Mother, you scared the dickens out of me."
She kissed my forehead and went to the garden.

"Where the devil do you think you're going? It's freezing out."

"I'm fine, hen. Just need some air."

"Well, at least take a cardigan. You'll catch your death out there."

Marnie

Izzy's reaction to Gene's death was totally unexpected. She wouldn't let us call an ambulance and lay there cuddling his dead body, stroking his hair and kissing at his cheeks like she really loved him. It made me sick watching her like that.

The next day when I woke to silence I thought she might have left in the night and done a runner like she always does. Instead I found Nelly in the kitchen sucking on cornflakes and Coke. When I asked where Izzy was she nodded toward the garden. I only had a T-shirt on and it was freezing outside so I grabbed a cardigan. We have a pervert living next door and the less he sees the better, but Izzy wasn't in the garden and the shed door was open so I make a barefoot run and that's where I found her, or where Nelly must have found her before returning to her fizzy cereal. Izzy had hung herself.

When I went back to the house Nelly was still eating. I told her Izzy was dead.

"Well, that's torn it," she said.

I explained what would happen to us if Welfare found out. She nodded. I told her we had to bury them in the garden.

"You think that's wise?" she said.

"Course it's wise, ya fucking balloon."

Before we buried them I checked their belongings for money. Gene had half a tab and some receipts. I don't know why he kept receipts. He also had a banker's card with his PIN, 4321, written on a label stuck to the inside of his wallet. Seriously.

Izzy had a handful of change and some fags, a telephone number, some sleeping pills, and some jellies, or benzos. I kept the fags and tossed the pills, but then I thought I might make money from the pills so I fished them back out of the trash and sold them on. I also kept her purse. I was there when she bought it. Calvin Clone. She also had forty quid. Thank God. We would have starved otherwise 'cause there was fuck all in Gene's account.

Nelly

Marnie makes me do things I don't care for. Says all kinds of ghastly things. Dead, buried, over, but must she go on? Beastly girl.

Marnie

Getting Gene off the bed and into the garden was a living nightmare. His face was swollen, as if someone had beaten the crap out of him, and he was sticky, like he was leaking venom. It was coming out his eyes, his nose, and his mouth. And the smell, I was gagging.

We decided to wrap him in the sheet he was lying on, we couldn't stomach the idea of touching him again, but it was soaked right through with this syrupy fluid and so we had to get another sheet and that did mean touching him again. Rubber gloves would have been useful, but we didn't have any. All we had were woolen ones, so we used them instead.

Gene's flesh was literally falling off him and ripping like paper in some places. Every time we moved him he made a noise, like a fart, except wet and by the time we'd reached the top of the stairs we'd had enough and couldn't bear to hold him any longer. At one point his arm escaped, limp as a rope, Nelly tried to cover it, but she accidentally caught his hand and his fingernail came away and got stuck in the knit of her glove. She boked then and couldn't take it anymore. Neither could I, so we mutually agreed to push him off the top landing and let him roll to the bottom. It was the worst thing we could have done. He burst at the seams, body fluid everywhere, on the carpet, on the walls, a swamp of poison.

"You beastly, beastly man," says Nelly.

We had to get a wheelbarrow in the end, stole it from the next-door neighbor, then we spooned Gene off the floor and took him out back.

Izzy was already in the shed, her eyes sinking into her head and her tongue hanging out, but still, she didn't look half as bad as Gene, more bloated and less green, a sort of damp blue color. When Nelly saw Izzy she burst into tears, then she threw up, I mean really threw up. I was on autopilot. I wanted them buried and gone. I didn't have time for tears, I knew we had a job to do and mostly I was wishing we'd got rid of them sooner and, to be honest, I don't know why we didn't.

We spent all night digging, the ground was practically frozen. It was tough to get the earth to move. We also realized there wouldn't be enough room for both of them in the grave, we'd forgotten about the earth we had to put back in the hole to actually bury them and since Gene was the smelliest of the two we decided he was to be buried first and Izzy we squashed into the coal bunker knowing she'd decompose but be accessible for the pouring of disinfectant when necessary. But a week later we had to scoop her into a bin bag and shove her under the shed because she was leaking across the cement.

Last thing we did was pour bleach over them; a lame attempt to disguise the stink they'd left behind, though Nelly insisted the cold would be enough to keep the stench at bay. Then we went inside to purge what remained of Gene from the stairs, but no matter how we scrubbed we couldn't remove his stain, though we scoured until the color left the carpet and the skin on our knuckles burned blood. That's when we decided to pull the carpet up and got a knife and ripped every inch of it from the stairs. But even with the carpet in the bin the scent of their death remained in the house.

When all was done we covered Izzy with two sacks of coal and planted lavender on top of Gene, not out of sentiment you understand, but to better hide what was buried in the earth. The saleswoman at the Garden Centre said lavender grows fastest and has a strong smell but worried about the weather being so cold, suggested we wait till spring. She said we only needed a few bushes, but they were so small we bought more. We needed to cover the grave. She also said that lavender attracts bees and not to plant it next to a door. Then she went on about how the honeybees were becoming extinct and how sad it was for the environment. Nelly was freaked by that and talked of nothing else for about a week. Eventually I had to tell her to shut the fuck up about the bees, which I felt bad about afterward, but she was really getting on my nerves and was constantly asking questions I didn't know the answers to. I mean I was making up all kinds of shit at first, the bees have migrated, the bees are evolving into another species, but then it got too hard and my answers were scaring her, I might have said something about global warming coupled with a nonsensical end-of-the-world theory, I don't know. She just makes you feel like you have to know the answer to every fucking question she has. In the end she gets me in a corner, goes right up to my face, not even asking anymore but demanding an answer, so I gave her one.

"I don't know a fucking thing about the honeybees, so stop asking," I say.

She stopped then, hasn't mentioned the bees since, not one word, but I know she still thinks about them.

Nelly

My father, a loathsome, malignant type of a fellow, sat me on his lap in the nighttime. Said he loved me.

Later I find him spent, stagnant, unclean, crumpled on an unmade bed. I find my pillow by his head and good golly Marnie had pushed it over his face.

And a good ruddy riddance to you, Eugene Doyle.

Marnie

I love my friends. What is real to them is real to me. We don't care what people think either and we've been holding hands since our primary school teacher told us it was the safest way to cross the road. We've been hanging together "that" long and there's nothing we don't know about each other, maybe there's a few things, but mostly we tell each other everything.

Susie lives with her granny. Her mum's in a loony bin. Susie's going to be an actress one day, she's brilliant at acting. Goes to the drama club with all the squares, not deliberately of course, she got caught smoking in the cloakroom before Christmas and instead of getting detention she was sent to drama club once a week for a month, now Susie's in the school play, *Oliver Twist*. She's Nancy, has tons of songs to sing. Kimbo and I said we'd help with costumes and stuff, but only so we can hear Susie sing. It's a pretty cool musical.

Miss Fraser (failed actress in vintage clothing) wants Susie to go to drama school. She's already spoken to Susie's granny about it, but her granny wasn't having any of it.

"Actress, that'll be fucking right," she says. "You're cutting folks' hair. It's a job for life, hen."

"S'not up to you!" Susie told her.

Her granny slapped her for that. "Don't you contradict me. Fucking madam," she says.

Susie was fuming for days, says her granny can go fuck herself, not to her face obviously, just to show us how serious she is about acting. She's even stopped smoking, only does it when she's drunk, says it's bad for the voice; so is coffee, apparently.

Izzy told me one time Susie's mum was a nympho. Would fuck a stick in the ground. It's a shame for Susie; her mum left when Susie was really small. Truth is Susie hardly remembers her, but loves her like she's in the next room. Sometimes Susie gets scared she'll end up in a loony bin too, like it runs in the family or something, and gets really depressed about it, but with all the support she's getting from her mates and from the drama teacher you can see the confidence in her growing by the day and she's starting to seriously think about life beyond Maryhill and a life away from her mad granny, who shoplifts by the way.

Kimbo's totally different from Susie. Everyone's scared of her 'cause she's bipolar, she got diagnosed last year. Her parents, dope-smoking fiends, didn't want her taking medication, if you can believe it, and insisted on therapy to help her handle her emotions, but when she threw a chair through the window of the school common room it became necessary. She's put on a lot of weight recently, nasty side effect of the antipsychotics she's taking, but apart from that they're working really well, although this one time she did go off them. She said she was feeling better and stopped taking them, but you can't do that, turns you into a psycho if you do that. She wasn't hospitalized or anything but she couldn't leave the house for a month. Susie and I prefer medicated Kimbo, everyone does, she's like Santa when she's doped, and always laughing and giving you stuff. I feel bad she's fat 'cause it's not like she's tall enough to carry it and of course she's totally deluded about it and wears clothes that are way too small for her. Before Xmas she got a belly button ring and it took the guy three stabs to make the hole, but she still doesn't get it and it's not like her parents are going to say anything, they worship her. Kimbo's maybe one of the few teenagers on the planet who actually likes her mum and dad. I don't blame her. Greg and Kate are brilliant; always knock before entering and when Kimbo tells them to "fuck off" then that's exactly what they do. If you go to Kimbo's around dinnertime her mum always makes you eat with them. It's usually McDonald's. Greg and Kate love McDonald's, although there was this one time I went round and they were having macaroni and cheese with tomatoes on top. Kate made it for Greg's birthday, he's mad for it apparently. She put a flag in the middle of it. He likes flags. I'd visit them every day if I could, but they live in the penthouse and I'm scared of the elevator. Also they like to walk around butt naked and sit with their bare arses on sofas and kitchen chairs. It's like Kimbo doesn't even notice anymore. Anyway that's how I know Kimbo and Susie. We lived in the same block. We were on the third floor, Susie on the first, and Kimbo was on the top.

When Susie and I moved from the blocks Kimbo transferred to the same school as us, that's how close we are. Izzy hated it in the towers and was glad to be rehoused. They moved us to Maryhill on Hazelhurst Road, newest housing estate on the block. I can still remember the smell when we got here, paint and putty, but I don't go round Kimbo's anymore. It's dangerous and not because of the refugees they've housed there but because of the wee radges who don't like the refugees there. Glaswegians are very territorial, even in a shit hole like Sighthill. It never occurs to them the accents around them belong to doctors and nurses, teachers and lawyers, educated people forced out of nice homes in beautiful lands only to be stored in tower blocks in the northeast of Glasgow. I mean seriously. Imagine losing everything you are and everyone you know, to have survived rape, starvation, and homelessness, to have escaped death at the hands of genocidal maniacs only to end up in a moldy housing estate. Now we have immigrants with university degrees and doctorates prostituting themselves, selling drugs and doing whatever they must to survive the hell we call asylum. I suppose the real heroes are the ones who come here and endure the food stamps, the local abuse, the secondhand clothing, and the poor housing, not to mention the mountains of paperwork needed to be acknowledged in a country that doesn't even know your language; but the others, the ones who turn to crime to survive, who form gangs to protect themselves from the daft arseholes who battered them senseless when they first came here, they fight a new enemy and with the same stealth that drove them from their countries in the first place.

There's this one guy called Vlado, a big man who drives a BMW 5 series and when I say big, I'm talking six foot four inches of the guy. He's not a main man, obviously; he works for someone with no connection to Vlado should the shit hit the fan. Kimbo's mum totally fancies him. Called him salty. He apparently comes to the block sometimes to hang with Kate's friend Sarah and not often, but enough to make Kate jealous. Kate said Vlado used to be a teacher. Now he's a supplier to fuckwits like Mick the ice cream vendor, who is supposed to receive and sell. Once he sells he gets a cut, then Vlado gets a cut and the rest goes to whoever Vlado works for. Kate said

Vlado lost two daughters and a wife in the war. She says they might be alive somewhere, but he's too afraid to find them and he's scared they might have been taken to one of the rape camps, but then Kate says a lot of things, she likes to gossip basically and in my experience she rarely gets her facts right.

Anyway about six months ago the elevator at Kimbo's place broke down with me inside. I was stuck for over an hour waiting for someone to fix the thing and I'm not good in enclosed spaces. I totally freaked out and when the doors finally opened, Kimbo's mum had to give me a joint to calm me down, her dad has MS. I stayed with them for a couple of days after that, stoned mostly and when it was time to go I walked down twenty flights of stairs, but when I walked out the door I tripped over my feet and cut my knee. I immediately pulled it to my mouth and sucked on the broken skin, but it was still nipping and then someone says, "You okay, sweetheart?" It's a kind voice, like Italian, but not Italian, that's when I see it's Vlado. He gives me his hand and pulls me to my feet. I dust myself down, fix my top, and give my bra a lift. I start gushing then.

"God, I'm such an arse. So embarrassed. Sorry. You're Vlado, right?" I give him my best smile, a little wave. "I'm Marnie." He says nothing for a moment, just stares at me, I can see his face darken then and he gives me the once-over. Head to toe. You know, the way men do. Except he's not looking at me like that. He's looking at something else and it makes me feel nervous and self-conscious, like he doesn't quite approve of me and it makes me fidget. I can feel myself redden, especially when he lets a whole minute pass.

"Go home to your mother," he whispers.

He's disappointed and I can hear it. Then he says, "And get

a Band-Aid for that knee," and then he walks away. His words sting for obvious reasons, but more than that, there was a kind of derision in his voice, a little laughter.

When I turn to the glass door I see a translucent self staring back at me. I quickly scan my appearance and search frantically for whatever it was that might have offended him, the black pumps, my ripped leggings, the graze on my knee, the pink letterman jacket I borrowed from Susie. I curse myself for not wearing heels, but I was walking down twenty flights of stairs, I would have broken my neck in any other shoes. I wonder if it's because I'm not wearing any makeup or any lipstick and I feel embarrassed then. I always try to look my best and on the one day I don't I crash into someone like Vlado. I haven't been round much since then. It's a shame really because you should see Kimbo's view, especially at night, the whole of Glasgow lights up like a Christmas tree, you could forget where you are with a view like that and if it wasn't for the constant echo of sirens and screaming in the stairwells, you probably would.

Lennie

I've been watching them for days now. Digging. Gardening. Hulking years of waste from the bottom of their scabby garden. A broken toilet bowl and a few traffic cones, a smashed-up TV and a rusted bicycle, a child's buggy and a ton of bin liners and full of crap no doubt. They're eager little beavers all right, they filled the stolen shopping trolley to the brim and afterward they planted lavender. French I think. It's a funny little plant lavender but it won't take, not in this weather, although I was impressed to see they planted it well and kept it in the pots, spread a little mulch and then covered it with plastic. I don't know how they moved the earth, it must have been ice solid. They're cleaning house it seems, there's laundry waving from the line and dirty water thrown from buckets, there's a lot of bleach and a lot of industrious noise, but no music. The youngest hasn't played in weeks now and I love to hear her play. Quite the talent.

Bobby hardly noticed of course, the noises I mean, not so much as a paltry bark. He's a little under the weather these days. I took him to the vet last week, he said he had mange. They gave him a bath and some antibiotics, an anesthetic for the pain but the poor thing can barely stand up. He sleeps all day. And the stink on him. He'd wake the dead. I'm starting to worry he might die. The vet says his sores are very bad and in some cases septicemia sets in. He said I've to feed him fish oil and rice.

I should have left him where I found him really. A little white stray. He's like a terrier and was shivering in the alleyway next to the bins, looking for a bite to eat. Such a small thing and so frightened. Your heart bled for him. I suppose there was no harm in taking him in, it just seems he's always ailing. The vet said to change his food. He says he probably has an allergy. I might do that. It wouldn't hurt to splash out a little I suppose; I've grown quite fond of him now. I couldn't bear it if he died.

I saw the girls using the infamous trolley and ridding themselves of years of filth, it made me think of last Christmas, the father pushing the mother like a baby in a pram. He was singing, remember? At the top of his voice. It was two in the morning. Flower of Scotland. Take the High Road. The Northern Lights. Songs he had no right to. Songs about heroes and warriors, songs about rebellion, about places he'd never been. The wife was clutching at a traffic cone, each of her legs hanging limp over the side of the cart. I thought she was dead at first, but then she lifts her head and leads it to a cigarette. That's when she saw me staring at them and made the usual stink about having a faggot for a neighbor. They threw some cans and a bag, her bag, the contents bouncing off the concrete. She tried to stand up, didn't she, and fell out headfirst. That's when the plumber who can't fix sinks showed up, he gave her a towel and that ugly wife of his was furious and yelling in the background, "Don't be getting involved, Tommy." Eventually the ambulance arrives with the police in tow, the plumber gives a statement and Mr. Eugene Doyle is taken away (to the cells most likely). The mother didn't get home till Boxing Day and with a big bandage on her head. I can't imagine what those girls did that Christmas. I can't imagine what they're doing this Christmas. I haven't seen much of the idiot parents, or heard for that matter. I should be grateful for the silence, but I'm not, it's all very unsettling tell the truth. Very unsettling.

Marnie

Christmas was awful. We found gifts from Izzy and Gene hidden in the broom cupboard. We were looking for the disinfectant to clean what was left of Gene off the floor. I got a stolen iPod. Nelly got a Harry Potter DVD. We also got jewelry. Gold cross for me and matching earrings for Nelly. They probably thought we could share them. I felt bad then, the crosses were nice but it felt like an RIP from the grave. There was a bracelet in there for Izzy from Gene, a gold charm bracelet, but I took the Xmas tag off and told Nelly it was from me. She was all over it, liked the charms.

We had some food in the freezer. A chicken stir-fry and a few oven fries. A totally pathetic excuse for an Xmas dinner but we didn't want to go out. We were suddenly scared of everything outside the house and so we ate what we had, mostly in silence and with our food on our laps, watching the telly. Nelly was sullen. At one point I turned the radio on but she freaked out and snapped it off. She's not really into music at the moment. She won't play, and sits still. I suppose it reminds her of Izzy, who liked to sing except she couldn't, it didn't stop her from screaming her lungs out though, especially when she was hammered, she'd crank the volume to nuisance level and the neighbors would lose their minds and call the police sometimes. I suppose if Nelly's reminded of Izzy, she'll probably start thinking about Gene and that's the last thing she needs or what I need. I'm sure she didn't mean to kill him, but it's done now and there's no point in dwelling. She has to move on. We both do.

We've so much at stake right now and I can't go into Foster Care, not again, it isn't safe and who knows what would happen to Nelly, they'd probably put her in some sort of nuthouse with her being so weird. God, I hate Foster Care, you have to share rooms with girls who nick your fags and steal your clothes. The meals are good though, but I hardly saw Nelly. They always had her in rooms with bricks and puzzles. She didn't say a word the whole time and kept doing that hedgehog thing, curling up into a ball and screaming. She was only nine, I was eleven. Izzy had run away with the Estonian guy from Milton Keynes and Gene was missing in action. Kimbo's mum offered to take us in, but the social worker said there wasn't enough room in her house. It was Nelly's fault we were there at all. She kept peeing her pants at school and so the Social turned up to find out why. I suppose she didn't grass, but when she acts out like that people get suspicious and next thing some guy and his clipboard's knocking at your door.

We got some chocolate for Christmas from Kimbo, that cheered Nelly up. She ate the whole box while I smoked about twenty fags. Then we watched *Only Fools and Horses* for the ten millionth time.

God bless Hooky Street.

Nelly

Silent Night. Holy night. All is calm. All is bright. Round yon Virgin Mother and Child. Holy infant so tender and mild. Sleep in Heavenly Peace. Sleep in Heavenly Peace. Silent Night. Holy night. All is calm. All is bright. Round yon Virgin Mother and Child. Holy infant so tender and mild. Sleep in Heavenly Peace. Sleep in Heavenly Peace. Silent Night. Holy night. All is calm. All is bright. Round yon Virgin Mother and Child. Holy infant so tender and mild. Sleep in Heavenly Peace. Sleep in Heavenly Peace. Silent Night. Holy night. All is calm. All is bright. Round yon Virgin Mother and Child. Holy infant so tender and mild. Sleep in Heavenly Peace. Sleep in Heavenly Peace. Silent Night. Holy night. All is calm. All is bright. Round yon Virgin Mother and Child. Holy infant so tender and mild. Sleep in Heavenly Peace. Sleep in Heavenly Peace. Silent Night. Holy night. All is calm. All is bright. Round yon Virgin Mother and Child. Holy infant so tender and mild. Sleep in Heavenly Peace. Sleep in Heavenly Peace. Silent Night. Holy night. All is calm. All is bright. Round yon Virgin Mother and Child. Holy infant so tender and mild. Sleep in Heavenly Peace. Sleep in Heavenly Peace. Silent Night. Holy night. All is calm. All is bright. Round yon Virgin Mother and Child. Holy infant so tender and mild. Sleep in Heavenly Peace. Sleep in Heavenly Peace. Silent Night. Holy night. All is calm. All is bright. Round yon Virgin Mother

29

and Child. Holy infant so tender and mild. Sleep in Heavenly Peace. Sleep in Heavenly Peace. Silent Night. Holy night. All is calm. All is bright. Round yon Virgin Mother and Child. Holy infant so tender and mild. Sleep in Heavenly Peace. Sleep in Heavenly Peace.

Marnie

I like to think he had a heart attack and did a ton of E or something. It happens all the time, but that's not how it happened, not for him. Nelly did it. With a pillow. The furry one with the princess on it. I found it next to his head. I don't know where she got the strength, to be honest; he was wasted no doubt, not even conscious most likely. If they ever dig him up, we can blame the E. Gene was always doing E. He said it made him feel like a better person without stealing his soul. After he quit heroin Gene was always going on about souls and chicken soup and roads less traveled, he was quite the thinker for a while and actually considered himself drug free when he swallowed a tab or took a jelly, even Valium made him feel a little superior over the losers he knew still chasing their dragons. Crystal meth was always a weakness, basically anything he wasn't injecting made him feel like he wasn't really using. He used to say, "I only do it now and then," but it was more now, then and later. I've been offered it a couple of times, easy to get hold of, especially in my circle and they always know who to tempt, like Jehovah's Witnesses and Hare Krishnas seeking out your sad stories, listening for hours like fawning friends, not to help or save you, but to possess you, to control you. Drug dealers work in exactly the same way. Charming. Interested, super-attentive to your needs, until you're hooked that is. I do E from time to time and a couple of jellies here and there, but that's all, it wasn't too bad, E makes you feel pretty good about everything for about five minutes, but then the feeling passes and you get so low you just want to die, maybe become a Hare Krishna and worship God with a vengeance.

Thinking a lot about God these days and I wonder if he's going to help the suffering children or punish them. I should have stopped Gene when I had the chance, I'm not sure if I had a chance, but sometimes I think I might have. I should have said something to Izzy, but I didn't, she wouldn't have believed me anyway and wouldn't have heard me. Even when I put the lock on my door she never asked why. Last time I touched him was when I was burying him. It never occurred to me he'd go after Nelly, we're so different.

Nelly

Grammy read us incredible stories, had a true sense of the dramatic. Grammy was a lady, a duchess perhaps, liked to drink bitter-smelling juices sweetened with lime and sugar. Stirred them quickly with hot spoons and forks.

A graceful woman our grammy, she said so. Carried age like cashmere, her scent drifting in whispers and folds wherever she went, unlike our mother, who preferred tight clothes and fun drinks, sooking them up with straws and slurps.

"A common type of person," said Grammy. "Uncouth. Grotesque. How I loathe to hear the woman yowl," she spat.

Grammy never yowled, her voice was pure. She read life from cards with Towers and Emperors, Knights and Queens. She told me the future. She told me not to be afraid. She told me I was "possessed of light and have a higher purpose."

Grammy would speak of lost things, old things, things we should remember when it is hard to love, when one should play.

"Music is a feast of love," she told me.

It's what she said.

Lennie

They're gone. The parents. Over Christmas if you can believe it. God knows where they are. They left for three weeks last time. Those girls are too young to be left alone, they're just children and yet not children. The oldest one sits out back almost every night, smoking mostly. Smoking and staring into absence. You want to reach out sometimes, but you daren't. I'd probably frighten them. Their parents certainly told them what to think of us. Two years we've been neighbors and not so much as a tired smile. I don't blame them. I'm the boogeyman round these parts, branded and known. You'd be ashamed of me, Joseph, so ashamed.

Marnie

It was Gene who started it, me working for Mick's ice cream van selling confectionery, except it's not just confectionery. He sells drugs. Anyway Gene owed him money and so I went to work for him to pay the debt off. Don't get me wrong. It's not a total hardship. Mick's all right. We understand each other. The only issue we have right now is Gene. I told him Gene had gone to Turkey with Izzy; he didn't like that and went mental. He banged his fists on the steering wheel. He's very protective like that. He calmed down eventually and said Gene was a prick and didn't deserve a daughter like me, and then he gave me a bonus, and told me to keep my eyes peeled if Gene showed up. I said, "No problem," and it really isn't.

Mick's wife's a hairdresser, her name's Julie. She just had a baby. Mick says it never sleeps. When he hired me he told her some sob story and made me out to be some charity case. Now she's always giving me stuff she hasn't washed 'cause I can smell her cheap perfume on everything and then she cocks her head to one side and goes, "Awright, darlin'? How's it goin?"

Hate her.

Mick says Julie's off her head. Unbalanced. He says if she ever finds out we're fucking she'll kill the both of us.

Lennie

I think about it every day. A man of my age seeking out rent-
ers in a public park. Using the dog as an excuse.

He'd approached me before, the young lad, he looked
around nineteen. I said no at first, but walking away from him
I knew I'd go back and so did he. I wasn't even looking for sex.
Just a voice. Any voice.

"Forty for a hand job, fifty for oral, and a hundred for the
other," he said.

I was silent for a few minutes and wanted him to repeat it.
He didn't. He knew I'd heard him the first time. I went for the
oral. Then the flashlight appeared and the renter did a runner,
so did Bobby and there was me sitting on a child's swing next
to the slide, my cock out for the world to see. The policeman
was disgusted. "Pull your drawers up, you dirty old bastard."
Then he read me my rights and led me to the police car. That's
when I saw him. A young boy, around sixteen, not nineteen at
all, but then I find out he's fifteen, an adolescent and wearing
mascara like a girl, bleeding black all over his face, like he'd
been crying, but he hadn't been, he wasn't the sort to cry, he'd
been running, his face wet with sweat. Freckles he had, little
orange freckles and a sadness so unfamiliar it chilled me. The
boy wouldn't even look at me and kept staring into the park,
he was trying to make me invisible. The policeman at the front

kept calling him Sandy and knew him quite well as a matter of fact. Asked after his mother. The boy was no stranger to them, a drug addict most likely, not that it helped my defense any.

The lawyer said the judge was lenient. "Most men in your situation go to jail," he said. "Three years minimum. Think yourself lucky." He told the judge I was a sad old poof with bad eyesight, which did the trick nicely, mostly because it's true. The judge gave me two hundred hours' community service, but was obliged to put me on the Sex Offender Register because of the boy's age. The real punishment was the neighbors of course. They kept spray-painting the door, and your sister wasn't best pleased either. She won't visit me anymore. It was an impossible thing to explain, especially to her. I don't even know how I would have explained it to you, connoisseur of the discreet; you preferred people to think of us as companions, which became easier as we aged, but I couldn't believe you didn't cite me as your next of kin. I had to get Sylvie to call the hospital and tell them I was a relative, they wouldn't have let me see you otherwise. Even on paper you denied me my place, you denied yourself. Fortunately Sylvie let me keep everything. She even gave me the insurance money. I gave her your father's cuff links. I thought she might like them for one of her boys. Decency came to her late in life. Let me make all the decisions about your care. She grabbed my hand after I signed the consent. She knew you belonged to me then and knew what I was losing, what we were both losing. While we waited for you to leave us she sat opposite me and we watched your pulse lessen on the generator, she held on to you as I did.

It happens fast when it comes for you, the callous quickening, the blood stilling, the breath falling swift as a swallow.

37

I held you tight then, bound you petrified to a life withering and anchored in silence, but you escaped me and a quiet calm embraced the room, a kindness drawing you close and letting you go. The passage of a gentleman.

Not many came to the funeral. Everyone we know is dead or in an old folks' home. There was me of course, your sister and her son and not the one in jail, the tall one with the black girlfriend, Belle's her name, but what's his? I always forget. I know the jailbird is Edward, but the blond one? Nice big bloke, John or Jo or is it James? I think it's James. Anyway they invited me to their place for dinner, but they never called. Sylvie must have told them about me and about the park.

The Abominable Albert was a no-show. He still hates a man even when he's dead. He simply refuses to accept James and Belle's relationship, even though they're expecting their first child in March and his first grandchild. Sylvie reckons he'll come round, but they don't care whether he does or whether he doesn't. Albert's a joke to them.

They're having their ruby wedding anniversary soon, down at the Bowling Club.

It would have been our ruby in March and I know you wouldn't approve, but I intend to celebrate it. I'm going to cut six roses from our garden and place them on your grave. I'm going to buy a bottle of champagne, expensive champagne, and open it right where you lie, then I'm going to drink it and maybe I'll cry. People walking by will only see an old man in a woolen coat and a sad little cap keeping his head warm. They'll assume Joseph William Grant is my brother, a cousin perhaps, maybe a friend, but probably a relative. They will misunderstand entirely because they want to, but if anyone should ask,

ask if I'm okay, I'll tell them. I'll say, "No, I'm not okay, my lover is dead. His name was Joseph and today would have been our ruby anniversary."

Then I'll go home half cut, ready to play the piano. I'll play Christmas carols and some Mozart, anything you loved. Then I'll fall asleep on the sofa and wake to a dog. He's all I know these days.

Nelly

When the music stops, the curtains twitch, the netting pulls and pinches. He's watching us from his windows, in a cardigan warm and woolen. He waters, clips, and prunes, all the times surveying, but I see him. He doesn't know that. No one knows that and I'll catch him. I'll catch the fellow.

Lennie

Made contact with the other side. The youngest mostly. Nelly's her name. I like her. She's such a nice girl, beautifully spoken, smells of clean linen and vanilla, unlike the older one, possessing odors not quite belonging to someone so young in my opinion. Marnie's her name and a very direct young lady she is too. She asked immediately about my past.

"You a perv?" she asked. " 'Cause everyone round here says you are."

I told her the truth. What else am I going to do? There's no point lying about it. Everyone knows anyway. Funny how she accepted it. I suppose she occupies a universe where such things are possible. She carries too much behind those green eyes of hers. It makes me sad for the girl, everything fresh and honest savaged from her hand by angry dogs, a childhood devoured. Nelly on the other hand holds tight to her infancy, seems more vulnerable; unfortunately she's growing into a woman and very rapidly in my opinion, like my cousin Sue, breasts at eleven and menstruating at twelve. Poor Sue. She never married in the end, and no kids of her own. Her mother was so afraid she'd get pregnant and took the life right out of the girl and so she stayed at home looking after her mum till she died. Afraid of her own shadow Sue was.

Nelly's a bright girl and plays the violin like a professional.

She was a little reluctant to play for me in the beginning, like she didn't have it in her, but the sister egged her on and told her it was important to play and so she did. Oh, how she shone and yet one can't ignore the sadness inside and the damage.

Nelly is an entirely different creature from Marnie. She seems less worldly in comparison. Nelly has a rather peculiar manner about her, like she swallowed a dictionary, not an unfavorable characteristic given the mouth I have to endure round here, but neither does it fit. She's an attractive girl, she turns heads wherever she goes no doubt, she has a great bone structure, I'm sure she'll get by. People tend to ignore the idiosyncrasies of the beautiful, but her strangeness, I expect they'll interpret it as an earned aloofness. Mostly the girl needs a parent. They both do. Poor things.

Nelly asked if I'd help with the lavender. I was reluctant at first, like I said, it's not going to take in this weather, but you don't want to hurt her feelings, also Bobby kept pulling up the earth and wouldn't come when I called him. The stupid dog, he can be very disobedient. And he keeps pulling up my ivy. I was also worried about their parents making a sudden appearance. The father would kill me. I went over anyway, skipped over as a matter of fact, it's so nice to talk to people and not many do round here. That's when the oldest showed up. I thought she might scream and yell for help, but she didn't. She seemed too tired to care. We had a chat about gardening and their lavender, my roses and the state of the street (it's such a mess right now). Then I invited them for dinner. They're obviously on their own and no one should be alone on New Year's Eve. They were a little reluctant at first and so they should be, but Bobby's happy tail must have told them it was safe and so they agreed and as things turned out we had a wonderful evening together.

Oh Joseph, to have someone to talk with and cook for, it was bliss. Marnie helped with the dishes and we talked. Nelly watched the telly and ate half the apple pie for dessert and a whole tin of custard. She must have been starving. That's when Marnie asked about the conviction and like I said, no point lying, although it still stuns me she was okay with it. She sort of shrugged it off as if it wasn't the worst thing she'd ever heard in her life and that made me uncomfortable because wherever she comes from she must know I took advantage of a child, of his poverty and his desperation, believing mine was more important. It doesn't matter that I didn't know his age, it wouldn't have mattered if he'd been twenty-nine. I was wrong. It makes me sick to think of it.

Marnie says her parents have gone to Turkey. She's asked me not to say anything and I won't. Nelly and Marnie are coming back tomorrow. They didn't ask, I offered. I'm glad of the company. I'll make a steak pie and some roast potatoes, peas, maybe a bramble and raspberry crumble. How you loved that crumble and I was so mean about it, I wouldn't give you the recipe in case you left me and made it for someone else. Doesn't matter now I suppose. The secret, my love, is lemon zest. I'd grate the skin of a lemon as fine as I could get it and I would do it when you weren't looking and then hide it on the top shelf of the cupboard under the stairs. I'd make crumble every New Year from fruit we'd gathered in the summertime kept frozen in our freezer, it became a tradition of sorts. It's been a long time since I've celebrated any traditions, how lovely to enjoy them again.

Marnie

With Gene fertilizing the garden, Nelly and I wait for it to grow, my sister and I aren't exactly blessed with green fingers, unlike the nosey child molester from next door. Yesterday he actually came over, reached out from behind the nasty gauzing he calls curtains. Lennie's his name, I got the fright of my life when I saw him at the bottom of the garden, his dog pulling at the lavender, thank God he put a lead on him. I don't know what Nelly was thinking leading him to the flower beds. She's such a moron. Anyway turns out he's not a pervert at all, just an old queer who got his cock pulled by Sandy Lane. Old guy's full of remorse, full of shame and at one point I thought he was going to cry. I felt a bit bad for him, but only a wee bit, he's still a perv if he's paying for sex. When he described the boy who gave him the wank I almost choked. "Young lad with red hair, not even sixteen," he says. I knew straightaway who it was. Of course Sandy Lane isn't his real name, his real name is Sandy Simpson, we just call him that because that's where he lives, in lanes and alleys, at bus stops and train stations.

We used to play together, me and Sandy. I totally bossed him about, like he was a dog or something, then one day he wouldn't play with me anymore, got himself a ball and kicked it around the stairwell. He made a lot of noise and got a lot of slaps.

His mum hung out with Izzy for a while. They drank wine in the daytime and listened to Britney in the evening. They had these daft bendy straws around their ears and pretended they were microphones, they had their shirts rolled up revealing two fat guts. Anne was her name, Sandy's mum I mean. She ended up in prison after she glassed some girl for snogging her boyfriend, except Anne's boyfriend was in the toilet. She took half the girl's face off. She did at least a year and that's when she joined the God Squad. She stopped using and woke up to a life she didn't recognize and Sandy, her only son, she didn't know him either and not 'cause she forgot.

Poor Sandy, he used to be so cute, red hair, blue eyes, and wee freckles, skin like a peach. He followed his mother around like a dog. He loved her the way wee boys love their mums, dependent and trusting, wanting and waiting, sitting outside pubs on pavements, rain or shine and for hours sometimes, eating crisps and whatever else was offered to him on the street. And the strangers. Sandy has reasons to hate his mother forever and couldn't care less about her repentance and likes to show up outside her church wearing a filthy tramp coat. He asks for money and begs at her knees, he calls her "Mummy" and says "please" and "forgive," he forces her to pull away and recoil. The parishioners know then. Who she is. Where she's been. What she's done. They understand why she sits in their pews staring at icons, seeking out judgment, seeking atonement for the boy still waiting for her on pavements.

Nelly

I'd hoped he'd be nice. He's delightful. An amusing type of a fellow and a real sport. He serves crumpets with curd and plays Beethoven and Bach. He is a fine pianist and we are quite the duet.

I admired his roses first and then his door, painted and glossed and with a brass nameplate. Our own door is bashed and broken, the window smashed and boarded. A dreary state of affairs. He smells of talcum powder, is possessed of china cups and matching saucers. How I love to hold a teacup. He uses side plates for breads and for cakes. It was all rather wonderful. Pristine. Polished. I played the violin later. Something forced upon me in the end. Marnie must always have her way you see and with no regard for one's temperament. If only she knew of my nightmares and of the dancing violin waking the dead from their slumber. If only she had seen them rise from their graves as I have, waltzing to a melody of my making.

Lennie

I've got a bad feeling about all of this.

The girls come round for their dinner every night. I don't mind that. I like it, you know me, I love to host, but tonight at dinner I noticed Nelly and Marnie exchanging funny wee glances, a collusion right over my apple pie, a slight of sorts brought about by a very casual inquiry on my part. I asked how long their parents plan on being away. It's been a month now, and when I think about it last time I saw them was around Christmastime before I went to the Loch.

I drove the whole way incidentally. I nearly killed myself. The weather was bloody awful. There was snow everywhere and the walk to the house? I thought I wouldn't make it. It's very hard to travel these days, but I don't mind. I've already seen the world. The Pyramids. The Hanging Gardens. The Eiffel Tower. The Leaning Tower. Ah, Italy. My Italy. The food, the architecture, the narrow little streets in Siena always leading to gourmet heaven. I could have lived there for the rest of my life, but not you, how you loved your Scotland. If I'd known you'd be leaving me in it I might have been more insistent about settling somewhere else. This country's a disgrace and the pensions you get these days? It's not much of a welfare state. Thank God I don't have to rely upon it, it's a scandal. If the poor buggers don't freeze to death for fear of putting their radiators on, they starve to death for fear of buying a slice of ham.

The cottage in Firemore was my consolation prize I suppose. We certainly generated enough memories there. If I wasn't on probation I'd move there tomorrow.

As for the girls, there's something they're not telling me. Maybe the parents are not coming back? Maybe something else has happened to them? Maybe they're languishing in a Spanish prison for smuggling drugs or some such. Who knows what kind of trouble those fools have gotten themselves into, but the girls know and they're not telling. I wish they would. I don't want to be caught unawares when the mother and father decide to make a show, but I'm getting the impression they might not be; coming back, I mean. They just don't mention them or make comments about them, even to say where they are or a bitchy remark, they must know I'd be open to it. It's as if they've erased them. If I'm being honest I just want to know how much time I have cooking dinners and listening to Bach, oh the delight Nelly brings to my home, I feel it is a beauty I don't deserve, but I need it, the color. Is it wrong to want to know how much time I have watching television with someone, reading to, caring about someone not you, not me, waiting up for Marnie (who is up to no good with the ice cream man by the way, I wasn't born yesterday and to think he does children's parties)? *Make your day special. Call Mick.* I'd have a word if it was my place to, but what is my place? I wish they'd tell me. Perhaps the parents are just having fun in the sun. Drunk on a beach somewhere most likely, just like last time, but it's been over a month now and that's odd, isn't it? I just can't remember when I last saw either of them. Not that

I miss them, but exactly how long do they plan to leave these children alone in the world?

I wonder if they'd like to go to the Loch during the school holidays. It'd do them the world of good, a nice trip away, it's beautiful in spring and in the middle of nowhere, but the peace, it's like no other place in the world. I could do with a break, I've been feeling a little under the weather these days and ever so forgetful. Of course if the bastard parents were to suddenly appear I'd be on the front page of the *Sun* for abduction. I'll run it by the girls. See what they think. Would be a tonic for us all, a real tonic.

Marnie

My guidance teacher Mrs. MacLeod (middle-aged yah trying to do good among the peasants of Maryhill) said the only thing keeping me from the abyss of total delinquency is my gift for learning. Like Nelly I apparently possess qualities that she believes to be wasted on a girl "so utterly destructive in temperament"—she actually wrote that in my report— meaning I smoke and drink and have abortions, actually one abortion, but still, I have an A average that I maintain with little or no effort on my part and they despise me for it, mostly because they can't take credit for it; in other words intelligence should be the reward of the virginal nonsmokers of the world, not some morally corrupt teenager with dead junkies in her back garden.

Even though I hate school, I still like to be there and especially after the holidays, which for me was always the worst time of the year, always having to deal with Gene and Izzy and their fucked-up Xmas Spirit. I like the orderliness of school. The routine. I find school bells strangely comforting and of course my mates go to school. Suzie and Kimbo. Not that I don't see my friends out of school, I do, but not all at the same time. School is a more convenient way for us all to congregate in one place, also we get free lunches.

According to Mrs. MacLeod I deliberately surround myself with "undesirable elements to sabotage my development." Of course Mrs. MacLeod knows fuck all about the elements around me and some of them I've had no choice over.

Anyway, before Christmas, MacLeod organized a "play-date" with Wendy Carter and Lorna Holland in an attempt to integrate me with the *desirable elements* of the school, girls who smell of white musk and toothpaste. We met at the library and we were supposed to form a study group. It was awkward as fuck and we had nothing in common. Their parents are accountants and lawyers and mine are buried in the yard. Anyway Wendy suggests lunch down at Burger King, which she very generously pays for and then we go for a walk at the Botanical Gardens. At first I was like, *God, this is going to be so boring* and then Lorna digs deep in her Louis Vuitton and produces a packet of fags and a hip flask with voddy and pomegranate juice in it, brilliant and we launch into a pretty good time, but then Lorna goes and ruins it by going on about the antioxidants in the pomegranate juice and how good it is for your skin and your weight, like that's why we're drinking it. Thing about Lorna is as soon as you relax in her company she geeks out on you and for about half a second you're thinking, *What the fuck am I doing here with this tube?* then she offers you a fag and you remember she's actually all right, but at the same time you're thinking, *She's still an arse.*

You certainly can't judge a book by its cover that's for sure, for a start the "desirables" aren't as "desirable" as they seem. I can't deny I was a bit shocked by the smoking and the drinking, like they're too privileged to smoke, daft really. It doesn't matter where you come from. We smoke because that's what we want to do, but it doesn't mean anything about who we are or what our futures are going to hold, but you get these teachers always seeking out troubled souls in cloudy bathrooms. It never occurs to any of these balloons that someone smoking on school premises isn't rebelling against the system, we're not even thinking about the system, we just want a fag. It's a survival technique, a lot of teachers smoke but no one's barging in the staff room judging their lives, their futures, putting them on detention.

Even though I have straight As, the smell of tobacco on my breath and an obvious lack of innocence gives them permission to shake their heads in dismay, as if disappointment and failure is a destiny I can't avoid. I bet they never shake their heads at Lorna, especially with her father writing big fat checks to the PTA fund-raising committee, people just don't couple wealth with neglect, idiocy with affluence. It's almost a waste of time having high marks when you're me and I wouldn't bother if it weren't for the fact I just always know the answer to everything, which is more than can be said of Lorna, who spends more time manipulating adults into believing she possesses the virtues I'm apparently without, when the truth is Lorna's an idiot and needs me to help her with a few academic issues she's having. She wants me to do her homework basically and said she'd pay me.

I'm not too sure how long Lorna's "desirable" status is going to last to be honest, she's like a bear in a glass cage. She's having a party this Saturday. Her parents are in Morocco. And who's the first person she calls on her mobile? Guests? No. Merry Maids? Yes. They're to come the next morning to clean up the mess she anticipates, foresight my second favorite characteristic next to insight. Talk about covering your deviant tracks. Definitely going to that party. Anything to get away from the smell in my house.

Nelly

What on earth is happening to the bees? They say it is an ecological disaster, an environmental holocaust.

Every day I wonder what the blazes can be causing this abuse of our ecosystem. Chemicals I hear, pesticides. I don't understand it, really I don't. Our planet faces extinction and yet nobody seems to care.

Am I afraid? You bet your bottom dollar I am.

Lennie

Nelly isn't strong. She's weak and easily bruised. Not one for screaming or shouting unless she's sleeping and of course there's the violin. I'd say she was beyond her years when it comes to her music. We've played some very pretty duets together; unfortunately I'm not the player I used to be and there are days I wonder if I can play at all. I don't know what's got into me this weather, I would forget my own head if it wasn't screwed on. She's practically a master of course and not at all like the sister, drunk every weekend, coming home in the middle of the night, singing at the top of her voice and attracting all kinds of attentions from the neighbors.

Wish Bobby would stay out of their garden. He'd dig the whole yard up given a chance.

Marnie

Kimbo and Susie turned up at the door tonight with a bottle of Tesco's finest red. Susie had cash she'd nicked from her granny and was ready to get wasted. I'd already sent a text saying I was sick and I am, if you count a hangover. Lorna's party was out of control. I don't remember much and woke up in Lennie's house. He was in a chair next to me, a bowl of sick at his feet. He made me drink a raw egg and I puked my load, but I felt better after. Then he made me a bacon sandwich and some tea. Nelly stayed out of my way, which is a good thing because she's driving me mental right now. She's playing truant from school and getting us noticed.

I'm also worried I might be pregnant. I came home minus my nylons the other night, I couldn't find them anywhere. I asked Lennie if he'd put them in the wash and he got all shy and told me I didn't come home with my nylons on, I got such a brass neck. Now he knows I'm a total slag.

I don't think I had sex with anyone, maybe Kirkland "minging" Milligan. He's been after me for months, maybe he knows what happened to my tights? Prick!

Anyway Susie and Kimbo show up, Susie in fake fur and Kimbo in combat trousers. Susie asked if Gene was about and it unnerved me a wee bit when she asked. I said he was on holiday with Izzy. She wanted to know where exactly they'd gone.

"Turkey," I said. Then Kimbo said they were probably trying to get away from the smell. "This house reeks of bleach and shit." I told her we'd a bunged-up toilet. She didn't mention it again, but she's right, the stink of Gene is all over the place, even with this cold, it's like he's stuck to the walls. I didn't want to drink tonight, but I took a wee swallow anyhow. Susie was being boring and a bit sulky, you felt like you had to drink. She was also being nosey as fuck about Izzy and Gene. The wine worked a treat but then Susie spills some on her dress and because she wants to go clubbing she heads to Izzy's closet. I couldn't stop her.

I haven't been in Gene and Izzy's room for weeks and it was disgusting. Sodden sheets crumpled on a mattress still stained from Gene's dead body. Izzy's makeup sprawled all over her dresser and lids everywhere. Her underwear left on the floor from where she just stepped out of them. Ashtrays full of fag ends. A half-drunk bottle of vodka. Laundry everywhere and of course the other smell. Their smell. A rancid smell of baked nicotine and stale perfume, cheap deodorant and dry alcohol. It made me nauseated. I tried to open a window, I needed air, but it was too late. I threw up everywhere. None of us wanted to stay in the room after that and so Susie grabs the red pleather skirt from a hanger in Izzy's wardrobe and takes it to my room to try on. It fits like a glove.

Next thing Nelly walks in and sees Susie in Izzy's clothes. I thought she was still at Lennie's, and looking at Susie, I see what she sees. I see Izzy. Nelly totally freaked out and Susie didn't know what hit her. It was Nelly. Kimbo had to drag her away by the hair, but then Nelly broke free and had another go. I can't remember what I was doing, I know I didn't help anyone. Susie's face was all scratched and she had Nelly's saliva all over her. Izzy's skirt was ripped to shreds.

And this is why I didn't want them coming around. I knew something like this would happen, it's been looming for weeks. Nelly's been really weird, like psycho weird, and Kimbo, she thinks we have rats in the house. She said it as soon as we left the house. She said she can smell rats like some dogs can smell cancer. She reckons one of them probably died in Izzy and Gene's bedroom somewhere. If only she knew what had died in Izzy and Gene's bedroom.

Nelly

Not a ghost but a thief. How dare she steal my mother's clothes? How dare she wear my mother's clothes? She had no business. And Marnie standing there, like it was nothing. Scallywags. A box in the ears was exactly what the doctor ordered. How could Marnie take them to their room? How could she bring them to our house knowing what she knows? It's not to be borne. She put me in an impossible situation. Violence was entirely necessary.

Marnie

Gene was in and out of rehab for about two-thirds of his life. The last time was when Nana Lou came and locked him in his bedroom. He was such a scaredy-cat, calling for his mummy and shit. She never went near him except to feed him and maybe slap him.

Nana Lou taking care of us is the one thing in my childhood I remember best. I also remember her songs. She used to be a pub singer and sang on cruise ships after Gene fucked off. She had an amazing voice. She loved Billie Holiday and Ella Fitzgerald. Patsy Cline and Dinah Washington, stuff I'd never heard of before. When Gene got better they sang songs together all the time. Old songs mostly. I remember them dancing in the kitchen. I didn't even know Gene could dance. He seemed like someone else with Nana Lou, someone not Gene, and Izzy hated it.

When Nana Lou was leaving Gene threw her a party. He got a karaoke machine and Nana got everyone dancing the Macarena, total strangers, but it was fun. I can still do the Macarena. Susie and Kimbo were there too, we sang Spice Girl songs and drank shandy. Nana Lou liked it when I sang. She said it made her proud. Nelly wouldn't sing at all and no one pushed her to, she ended up falling asleep under the kitchen table next to Izzy's feet.

Izzy hated the party and sulked all night. Mostly 'cause she can't sing a note. It didn't stop her making an arse of herself though, singing some crescendo-ridden love song. I remember eyes narrowing in agony, some laughter, and Nana Lou hiding smirks behind a smoldering cigarette. Izzy was so embarrassed and locked herself in the bathroom and our guests had to pee in the garden.

Izzy was so jealous of Nana and not just her singing but because she could make Gene do things Izzy couldn't. Izzy said Nana Lou loved Gene in a way no mother should love her son, she said if Nana Lou had loved him less Gene might have been a better man. Nana Lou heard her and said zero. She always knew how to deal with Izzy. She knew when to speak and when to say nothing at all. Nana treated Izzy like she was an insect bite, the kind you can't scratch without making it itch worse. I don't know what she made of Nelly, she liked to read to her and teach her how to be still. Nelly wiggles her leg a lot, especially when she sleeps. One time Nana Lou took us to Rothesay on the *Waverley*. It's a paddle steamer. We were on the Clyde, just sailing and she said, "Silence is power, girls." It was an amazing thing to say and I can't remember why she said it, but I never forgot she did. "Look at the water," she told us. "If it could talk you'd like it less." I liked the things she said. I liked having my hair stroked, my skin admired, and my stories listened to, being seen and being loved. Even now, after all these years, Lou's words mean more to me than the words I'm thinking on now.

Lou stayed with us for six months, she was supposed to stay longer, but someone called William got sick. Gene was furious.

He didn't like whoever William might have been. I remember they had a fight about him and Lou cried, but then they made friends. About a year later Izzy told us Lou had died. She had a heart attack. We never went to the funeral, Izzy wouldn't let us and neither did Gene, he was in prison at the time.

Nelly

Our phone died. Just like that. We can't call the local constabulary and we can't call an ambulance. Have you ever heard of such a thing? A calamity and no mistake.

Where does all the money go, that's what I want to know? Mother and Father left us something surely. A pittance I have no doubt but enough for groceries I imagine, some electricity, a little gas, and most certainly a ruddy telephone bill. She needs to manage the cash better is what I'm thinking. She needs to count her pennies and not her pounds. She needs to get clever with our budget.

"Maybe we don't need a phone?" she said.

"Goddammit," I cried. "Everyone needs a phone."

Blasted girl.

Marnie

Thank God for Pay As You Go, although Nelly doesn't share my enthusiasm and acts like I shit money or something. She never asks how we're getting by and just assumes we have it. Thank God for the welfare state and parents with sense enough not to marry each other. Izzy always wanted to marry but Gene said no and so that means two checks from the Social but for how long?

They talked about it a lot, being married I mean, and Nelly would get very excited, not quite getting that they were totally pissed and kidding her on. Izzy would draw wedding dresses and Nelly would find plastic rings for Gene to give to Izzy. They even went as far as to take the net curtains from the windows and stole flowers from Lennie's garden for a bouquet, but it was Gene they made up to be the bride. It was so stupid, Izzy and Gene wandering around half cut wearing curtains, Gene with his makeshift veil kept in place with a tin colander, which I suppose was his tiara, and Nelly trailing behind them in a mermaid costume. It was a stupid game. Scared me in my stomach having to pretend like that, but I still did it, just to throw the rice at them. They thought I was playing along, but I wasn't. I would have drowned them in rice if I'd got the chance and stuffed their every orifice with the stuff.

Nelly's acting like nothing happened with her and Susie

and Susie's still in a radge about it, even though Nelly apologized because I fucking made her. Kimbo asked me if Nelly was a schizophrenic, I said she isn't, because she's not. She doesn't hear voices or anything, she's just not like other people and can't fake it, which is more than can be said about me. I've been faking it my whole life.

Lennie

Alone soldier is our Marnie. It's all push and pull with this girl. She wants you, she likes you, she's afraid to be around you.

A boy keeps calling and won't leave his name. He obviously likes her and I can see why he would. Marnie's a very pretty young lady, but not in the same way as her sister. Marnie has a rounder face. They're chalk and cheese to tell the truth. Marnie wears makeup, pinks and reds. Nelly won't even wear lip balm, which is strange because I thought women loved to experiment with the lipsticks and the eyeliners. My sisters used to love a bit of rouge. We all did, but it was just a game. I would wear my mother's housecoat and her curlers and we'd all laugh and tease her, I'd wave my finger in the air and nag as she did, but how my mother raged about it. She always knew about me. How could she not? I wasn't exactly flamboyant in my way but it was clear I had no interest in women and from a very early age. I know my sisters knew about me. I was always the one they confided in and we were very close for a while, until I wasn't a secret anymore. It wasn't fair of them at all. I stuck by them, didn't I? Jeanette and her abortion, Roberta and her affair with the married carpenter. It was always me they turned to with their troubles but when I was the one who needed a friend they simply turned their backs. I never forgave them for that and made a point of keeping them as far from me as possible. It was a lonely time, I missed them all. I still do, but then I met you, didn't I? My brother. My lover. My salvation. I'd hate to have walked this road without you.

I am glad the girls have one another, it's a lonely journey otherwise and so I leave them with their secrets and the things they share. It bonds them and keeps them strong. It is important to stay strong, it ties you to life and forces you to walk on, even if it's only with a dog.

Marnie

Happy Valentine's Day, got one from Kirkland Milligan, who I thought might have been the one who shagged me when I was drunk and lost my tights at Lorna's shindig. He was totally offended when I asked him and told me I'd snagged my nylons on a chair and pulled them off by myself. He said I threw them at someone. To be honest I sort of blanked out after the karaoke. I remember Susie singing. Susie takes her karaoke very seriously, like she's expecting Simon Cowell to drop by. She's a little depressed right now. Susie gets like that sometimes, but she's darker these days and doesn't want to go out like she used to. Kimbo says it's 'cause she's an artist now and wants to hone her creative energy for the stage. Susie told Kimbo to go fuck herself. See what I mean—dark. Anyway Kimbo, me, and Lorna sang really badly, but we were just having a laugh. I got steaming at that party and made a right arse of myself. I started singing without the karaoke machine. Some of Lorna's bitchy pals from Kelvinbridge started sniggering at me, but then Susie joined in, making my song sound better and then Kimbo joined in, making it sound loud and then Lorna joined in and suddenly we weren't singing at all, just screaming, like our mums do when they're pished, I don't think the other party guests appreciated it too much, but we were laughing so much at it we didn't care. Kirkland sang some soppy song and kept pointing at me when it got to anything to do with love or hurt or being fucked-up in general, which made Susie and Kimbo piss themselves. He didn't care he was making a tit out of himself, I mean everyone knows I'm not interested. Susie thinks I'm being a bitch. She said people should be grateful when someone wants to love them and it's fucked up when they're not.

Kirkland's okay I suppose, but he wears a lot of black and never washes his hair, he says it cleans itself after a while. He has this raw sensitive thing going on and is always selling you the notion he's someone you can trust, but the truth is he's just trying to get into your knickers like every other guy. He keeps making me CDs of bands he thinks I've never heard of. He has a New Order thing going at the moment and he's always telling me what the songs are and what they mean. What he doesn't know is Izzy pure loved New Order, when they were New Order of course 'cause they used to be Joy Division according to Izzy.

I want to say all these things to him and put him in his place but then he'd think we had something in common and I don't want to have anything in common with Kirkland and so I assume inferiority in the hope he'll leave me alone. I nod a lot at Kirkland and hope he'll go get me a drink 'cause I can't be bothered going over to the bar. He never does though. He thinks he's that interesting.

The other thing I hate about Kirkland is his belief he's a humanitarian, he's always talking about Afghanistan and Iraq, as if knowledge makes him brave, as if caring and talking about these places is equal to actually being there and fighting the rebels he hates so much, he'd totally shite it if he had to go to war.

He's a pain in the arse to be honest and assumes you can't know whatever it is he knows. He's the type of person who loves the idea of being an outsider because he thinks by not belonging it makes him superior in some way. What he doesn't get is that the real outsiders would do anything to be on the inside. A real outsider can't be seen at all. They're people who look like they belong when inside they know they don't. They're people who would do anything to appear normal, while harboring the secret knowledge that they're anything but normal.

It probably sounds like I hate him. I suppose I do, the array of choices available to him bugs me. The only reason I know him at all is because he used to go to school with Lorna, but then they kicked her out and now she goes to our school, but he's still hanging around her and so are we these days. Kimbo and Lorna are pretty tight. Both of them want to be artists and they spend hours in her studio and I don't blame them. Lorna's house is amazing. I've never seen a place like it. A town house on Great Western Road with three floors, a private road with parking. Lorna has the attic. It's like a studio with its own entrance. Her parents let her do what she wants, and not because they're dead but because they work. Her dad's a barrister and her mum, not her real one, is a legal secretary. Lorna hates her. I'm stuck with Susie at the moment and her inane interest in Gene and Izzy. I've told her they're on holiday, but she wants to know when they're coming back. She says she's worried about me being alone. I told her I wasn't alone. I have Nelly. Her and Mick are both making me mental right now, totally fascinated by the disappearance of two complete nonentities. Why do they even care? It's not like they don't have enough to do. Susie's Nancy in the school play and Mick has a shitload of drugs to sell. He seems really pissed off at me right now, like it's my fault and I suppose it is in a way, but not like he thinks.

I've been washing the floors and walls all morning. I still can't get the smell of dead out of the house, although Nelly insists she can't smell anything. I even washed the linen in their room. Cleaned it up like they've never left, but the mattress still has a stain on it and whatever was leaking out of him has gone right through. I suppose we shouldn't have left him so long. I suppose we shouldn't have done a lot of things.

Anyway my hands are pained with bleach and I can hear Nelly playing the violin for Lennie. I'll go over later and have some breakfast, I don't like it over here.

Nelly

Cards given to me by strangers and three of them. One with a dog and a heart. One with flowers around a heart. And a flashing heart that sang a funny little song about roses. All from boys I barely know.

"Kip says to give you this," says Shirley.

"Matt says to give you this," said James.

"Patrick says to give you this," said Margo.

"Love you," they wrote over and over again. I felt sick and threw them into the nearest bin. How dare they send me such things? I am a student of merit. I have no time for cards and whatnot. They should save their money for more noble causes and leave me be.

I think on the word a while, *love*, and recall Grammy locking Father in the attic without his wine or his blasted teaspoons. I remember it well and with the greatest of accuracy.

"I do it out of love," she said as she put the key in her trouser pocket.

It was December. Almost Christmas. I remember Marnie in a Nativity smacking the Mother of God with a coat hanger. And Father, I remember Father dragging a man away from Mother. Mother said he was a villain but my grammy told me that it was my mother who was the villain.

"Have you no shame," cried Grammy. "And with two children in the house."

Mother wept at this.

I often wonder about my mother's shame and think of the balding stranger weeping blood around her feet.

"A painful slut." Grammy sighed.

"Well, you should know," spits Mother.

When Father left with Grammy (and the local constabulary) Mother sang a song. A song that made her feel strong, a song that made her feel sad, and a song that made her dance. I believe I danced too, I think she may have made me and I'm not at all inclined to exaggerate.

Marnie

I could have killed her.

I get home Friday and there's Big Brian, truant officer extraordinaire, waiting for me with a letter for my parents, which he wants to hand deliver. Then he gives me a lecture about skipping out of school even though it's a free period, reminding me it's actually study time and gives me a pink slip, which means I need to go see the headmaster on Monday so he can tell me the exact same thing, even though I'm an A student and don't need a study period. He then questions my parents' whereabouts and knows they're on the dole and says he's been trying to catch them at home for over a week and basically, where the fuck are they? He even hints they're working somewhere, in other words, collecting benefits while in employment and like it's his business, it almost makes me laugh, the idea of Izzy and Gene getting up in the morning to get to an actual job is fucking hilarious. I think of something to say without arousing suspicion. I tell him we have a dog and they must be walking it and then I suggest he wait longer for them like I'm expecting them any minute knowing it's Friday, and he wants to get home before the traffic fucks him and so he says it's not necessary and just gives me the letter.

Obviously he knows I'm going to open it and he doesn't want me to bin it so he tells me my parents have to report to the school administrator by the end of the month to set up an appointment or further action will be taken against them, which means I definitely can't bin it. Then comes the weirdest thing ever. He says, "Are you okay, Marnie?" I say, "Yeah." Then he says, "You know if you ever need anything you only have to ask, we're not the enemy, keeping a girl like you on track is important to us, do you understand?" I nod. He gets into his car and before he leaves he says, "Have a nice weekend." Then he drives away. I want to cry and wonder why he cares. Then I see our front door all bashed up, it's always been like that, but it's like I'm seeing it for the first time and it depresses me. There's plywood where a window used to be, I remember the stereo flying through it and there's a broken fence surrounding a junk-filled yard with gym equipment no one ever used. A cardboard box piled with clothes, shoes and total crap strewn everywhere. We did our best to tidy it when we buried them but it was too much. I look to Lennie's place with his perfect lawn. I look to the houses in front of us with kids' playthings and a bike against a wall. I see order and containment. I see homes. I feel ashamed and I want to fix everything, and make it look like it should. I know it's impossible. I go inside and rip open the letter instead and that's when I find out Nelly's been skipping school and more than I realized. The letter says Izzy and Gene can be made legally accountable and the word *accountable* is underlined.

Next thing I hear Nelly's key in the lock and so I position myself at the side of the door so I can grab her and kick the shit out of her. She gets a fright when she sees me and doesn't know why I'm home. I tell her I have a free period and she says, "It's not a free period, it's study time."

"Don't you fucking. Fuck . . ." I can hardly get the words out.

"What on earth's the matter with you?" she says.

"You getting letters like this!"

I throw it at her.

"I'm afraid there's been a misunderstanding, old girl. I'm always at school."

"Oh really, 'cause according to this you've been bunking off."

"I have not been 'bunking off,' as you call it. I've been reading. In the library. The school library."

"You're not supposed to be in the library, Fannybaws, you're supposed to be in class."

"I learn a great deal more in the library and without all that hullabaloo one must endure in a classroom full of imbeciles."

That's when I bang her. I've had it with her and the Bette Davis bullshit.

There's blood everywhere and a tooth is broken, but I don't feel bad, as a matter of fact I wanted to hurt her some more, she's lucky I didn't.

Later I go to see Mick and we have sex. I wish we hadn't and I feel disgusting afterward. I always feel disgusting with Mick. I don't know why I do it at all. Mostly I wish I hadn't hurt my sister, who ran from me in tears. I didn't mean to make her afraid, but she started it. I'm terrified now. There is no one to go to at school and they'll call again. I don't know what to do.

Nelly

Marnie gave me a right bashing. Thumped me and no mistaking it and on a Friday of all days.

"Whatever have you done to my tooth?" I cried.

"Fuck you," she replied. Vulgar girl. Uncouth.

Lord, how I hate Fridays. They can't be trusted. Weekends without supper, weekends listening to strangers brought home by careless fathers who drink and then pee on the bloody rug.

What a stench it leaves. An awful stench.

I feel badly for playing the fool, really I do. I don't wish to have government officials on the doorstep any more than Marnie does. I wish only to read and to stay away from the boys and their remarks about my body. I hate my body. I hate boys and today I hate Marnie. God damn her to hell.

Lennie

I gave Marnie a right talking-to yesterday and I was very stern. We had to take Nelly to the dentist. Marnie knocked the poor girl's tooth right out of her mouth. I had to control my temper, I really did, but then she started to cry. She says she's sorry and doesn't know what came over her.

"I want to know what's going on," I said.

"I don't know what you mean," she says.

"Your parents. Where the hell are they?"

She went blank, like she didn't hear me. I turn round to find Nelly staring at her, all wide-eyed and pleading and wanting her to keep her mouth shut. Marnie looked ashamed. They both did. I shook my head in disappointment and walked out of the room. There's nothing to be done if they don't trust me with what I already know. The parents are not coming back any day soon and these girls have been abandoned.

Later I chastised Marnie for her violence toward her sister, expecting some kind of teen-like strop and fully intent on throwing the little madam out on her ear, but she agreed with me, just like that. She was grateful almost, as if she wanted me to parent her and that's exactly what I did. I told her to apologize to her sister. She apologized, but Nelly wouldn't look at her of course and I didn't make her, I can't force her to forgive if she doesn't want to. I told Marnie to clean my kitchen. I'd been baking bread and had left a bit of a mess, but credit to her she cleaned the kitchen. Then I demanded she clean the toilet and she cleaned the toilet. I made her bring me her schoolbag, a sad little green satchel inked with boys' names and rock bands. I made her do her homework and it didn't take her very long but everything was correct. She's clever, I'll give her that. I let her have dinner, but no dessert, I told her she had to stay here tonight and go to bed early. She asked if she could have a bath. I said yes. She didn't as much as grumble, not once, that in itself is strange. It wasn't even eight o'clock, I expected a little backchat at least, but not a word did I get, only compliance and that's when I realized she wants someone to discipline her and to give a damn about the things she does right or wrong. And it hits me. These girls aren't hiding anything, this is how it has always been for them. Their parents' absence is a horrendous reality and one they have lived with their entire lives. I feel sore for Marnie then and for Nelly and suddenly I understand Marnie's attachment to girls like Susie and Kim. They are constants in her life. A family of sorts, something to look forward to and people she can rely upon.

After her bath she goes to bed as directed and I bring her milk and the shortbread I had denied her earlier. Nelly wasn't happy with any of these attentions. She sought retribution and when she didn't get it she sulked. Later I pulled her to the side.

"Your sister needs you," I told her.

"I care naught for what she needs."

I don't know what to say about that and so I go to the bathroom and pick up Marnie's towel and her laundry and that's when I come across her underwear, rolled into a ball inside her skirt pocket. I feel an enormous weight fall upon me then because I really don't know how to protect Marnie from Marnie. I really don't know.

Marnie

Jesus, Lennie let me have it the other night and has been a little cool with me since I smacked Nelly. I told him I was sorry, but I don't know if it was enough. I was so embarrassed in the morning and went home for a liquid brunch. Voddy with cranberry juice. Take the edge off. Asked Susie to join me but she was rehearsing at Drama Club and Kimbo was in Partick looking for a flat with Lorna. Lorna's parents have asked her to move out. They sent her to a psychiatrist recently, but it totally backfired 'cause after two sessions he wanted to counsel the whole family. Her mum and dad fired the guy. Poor Lorna, I thought she had everything, but it turns out she's as neglected as the rest of us. They're quite sweet together, Lorna and Kimbo. Lorna likes to lie with her head on Kimbo's lap and Kimbo likes to play with her hair. I think they're in love. Susie hates it and thinks Kimbo isn't taking her meds and being gay is some kind of symptom. She actually said their relationship was abnormal, this from a girl who has spent many a Saturday night on her knees and with guys she hardly knows, although not so much recently. She's like a nun this weather, less slutty than usual, but what a mood she's in.

Seeing Mick tonight. He's really pissed off right now. He thinks I'm hiding something about Gene; I am, but not in the way he thinks. He's super-anxious and always on the phone to Julie, they owe a lot of money. She's going nuts over it and won't leave him alone. We work till two in the morning some nights and so far no one has quizzed the ice cream van selling cones into the early hours of the morning. It seems I'm working for Vlado these days and I always make sure I'm looking my best, but he's still looking at me like I'm shit.

Gene and Izzy had their benefits stopped ages ago 'cause they weren't around to sign on. The money working the van was enough in the beginning, but then the Housing Association canceled the rent checks and now we're totally fucked. Moving isn't an option for obvious reasons and so one way or another the rent has to be paid. Delivering for Mick gets me around £150 a week. He also gives me a few tabs when I need them. I prefer a drink to be honest and so I sell them on to Kirkland mostly.

It was so nice at Lennie's the other night. I know he was pissed off at me, but he soon simmered down and brought me milk and shortbread. It's all it takes sometimes, something sweet. He's also agreed to go to school and sort the truancy notice Nelly got. He's been a real lifeline to us and we'd be nowhere without him.

After the shortbread and milk I went straight to sleep, but then I woke up and the agitation started. I felt like I had to get away from all the comforts and kindness, I'm not used to it and it makes me scared. He's making it too easy to stay and this makes it harder not to tell him what we're hiding in the garden.

Lennie

Nelly's still having nightmares. I can hear her through the wall. I gave her the spare room. She doesn't like to be alone in her house. I don't blame her, it's a tip. No wonder Marnie's always out with her friends. One of them is a dyke, which rather surprised me. They're all so very sexually assertive these days and at such a young age. Kim's her name. To be honest I can't be doing with the lesbians. They can be very difficult. Always seem to be in a rage about one thing or another, I suppose in a lot of respects it's easier to be a gay man than a gay woman, so much expected of women. I imagine your average straight man feels if women aren't women then how can they be men. They're very hard on the lesbians, the straight men; gay men are just irritated by them. I found it amusing the way Kim talked to me, like we were gay comrades, like we were men almost. I was pleasant enough about it but desperately wanted to remind her she was a woman and tell her it's okay to be feminine and gay, of course some of them feel safer occupying a more masculine role in life. Kim's certainly close to Marnie and probably loves her. Wants her. You never know the basis of a friendship when you're dealing with your differences, you know, in the beginning, when you start to realize who you are. I remember attaching myself to a boy named Toby, we were fairly pally for a while, but I didn't like him much. I just wanted to touch him. He married an old sack called Lillie in the end. I don't know what happened to him after that.

Nelly is the one I worry for, always crying through the nighttime, like you did when your brother died. Poor David, such a young man. Climbing in Milngavie. Not even that old and in his fifties. The wife followed soon after. Cancer.

They've asked me to see Nelly's headmaster Monday, they want me to pose as an uncle. She's been skipping school apparently. Marnie agrees the pretense is necessary but I'm worried about the consequences. What if someone were to recognize me? I could get into a lot of trouble. A lot of trouble.

Nelly

I sleep as sound as a pound most nights, but last night, what a racket there was, a lot of shouting and jeering on our doorstep. I couldn't make out what they were yelling, I really couldn't; drunks no doubt. At first I wondered if the truth had been discovered, I wondered if they were coming to incarcerate us for our wrongdoings, but no, they were simply disturbers of the peace, people with no regard for the slumber of others. I ought to have called the police but one didn't want to waken Lennie.

The next morning when I woke (and a little later than I intended) I found Lennie painting at his fence and his door. He's such a meticulous man but I can't deny the smell pained me somewhat, but if it needs doing it needs doing and there's nothing more to be said. Cleanliness is next to godliness after all and we all have to be clean, don't we.

Marnie

Lennie's been getting shit recently from the locals. Truth is he's always getting shit but last night there was some abuse in the early hours and then someone spray-painted his door and his fence. He just got up next morning and painted over it and even though he knew that I'd seen it he never mentioned it to me and so I said nothing about it either. I don't have a clue what Nelly made of it, probably what she wanted to. She's over at Lennie's all the time these days. She lives there and creeps in through the back almost every day and eats his food, sleeps in his spare room, and plays her violin. He loves it of course, having someone to take care of and for obvious reasons Nelly loves it too.

I suppose it's hard taking care of yourself at her age. You try not to think about it and pretend you're like everyone else who's twelve, but deep down you know you're not. You're alone. You need to heat your own home and pay your own bills, wash your own clothes and dry your own tears. No wonder she seeks this old granddad with his house smelling of baked bread. Lennie loves her like a granddaughter. She needs that, affection, warmth and not in a house smelling of bleach and death. The other day I actually chastised myself for leaving Gene in the house for a week before burying him, it was like a postscript to self. Bury people immediately.

Lennie's starting to suspect something and so is his stupid dog. He's always sniffing about the flower beds. I caught him the other day frantically flinging dirt between his paws, he actually pulled up Gene's arm, just like that, and I totally shat myself. Fortunately no one was around and I was able to replant the arm. I gave Lennie's dog a well-earned kick up the arse for that. He gave a wee yelp and Lennie appeared from his kitchen holding a dish towel. I don't think he saw.

"All right, Marnie?"

"Bobby's digging at the lavender. Lennie, can you call him?"

Despite a boot in the hole I find the little shit sniffing about the shed where Izzy is, but then Lennie calls him and he trots off. Disappears through Lennie's French windows.

"Dinner at five, Marnie?"

I nod, I love his dinners, but still, I might have to kill his dog.

Lennie

I went to the school posing as Uncle Leonard. There I met some woman with bad teeth. Mrs. MacLeod. Lots of ethnic jewelry. Wood and turquoise all over the place. She wears that patchouli oil and smelled like a bloody church. She was all smiles of course and very keen to support the girls on their "educational journey." The shite they talk in schools these days, it beggars belief. We discussed Nelly's truancy of course, which I assured her wouldn't happen again. She can't be missing school. Absolutely not. School is the one thing these girls have got going for them. Anyway we agreed on one week of detention for Nelly, which I felt badly for afterward but if it keeps her in school then it has to be done. She's also to report to this Mrs. MacLeod every morning. She won't like that much, but what can you do? If she doesn't stay in school it'll be the Social Work Department turning up at the door wanting to know the reason why and not this Mrs. MacLeod. No one will want to talk to Uncle Leonard then, that's for sure.

We talked about Marnie next. She was especially keen in this respect. She even went to the trouble of showing me Marnie's school work. All As and A pluses. Can't say I wasn't shocked. I haven't seen the girl study once, come to think about it I've never seen her so much as hold a book, just that bony wee arse of hers running to catch buses or jumping into the back of an ice cream van. The teacher said Marnie has an attitude problem and I'm thinking who the bloody hell cares. With grades like that she can be an armed robber. I don't know why the woman should give two hoots about the girl's temperament, but it's all very different in the schools today. Personality, cultural diversity, they even teach Gaelic, though I can't see what bloody use they'll have for it, not a great deal of Gaelic spoken in Scotland these days. They should be making them learn Spanish and French, German even, world languages, exciting them to participate in real causes, world causes, to confidently travel abroad and be able to ask for a bacon butty in Peru, but that's Scotland for you, always waddling about in the muds of yesterday, a parliament prioritizing a language spoken in places without work opportunities, wee islands where they raise cows and marry their relatives. I don't know. You can bring the horse to the water, Joseph, but you can't make it drink. Anyway the teacher then asked where the parental scum are and I tell her they're on holiday, then she wanted to know how I was related to the family and I told her I was the mother's uncle through marriage, twice removed. She seemed to accept it. There was lots of smiling.

It was an hour before she let me go, I had to sign something to say we'd had our "conference," the "conference" being a meet and greet in a musty old classroom smelling of felt-tips. Did I mention they're not using blackboards anymore? They use "whiteboards" now and they scribble on them with these big thick markers. Must cost a bloody fortune in pens.

On my way out I got a chance to wander the corridors. School smells never change, do they? Disinfectant and gym shoes is the stink they're possessed of, but no chalk smells, shame. I saw the fourth-year art display, a lot of jugs with apples, a pair of ballet slippers with a rose, and a nice tapestry of a ladybug. To tell the truth I was glad to get out of the place and when I did I saw this huge poster of a carving knife with a cross through it. NO WEAPONS, it said. Then another, like a traffic sign: NO DRUGS ON SCHOOL PREMISES, with a picture of pills and needles and a cigarette burning. Honest to God, it would make your head spin off its shoulders.

I wonder about these kids. Take that Kim for instance. She's gay and not even eighteen and has freedoms I could only dream of. I could never have told my parents I was gay at eighteen, they'd have died of shame, it was information trickled toward them and over many years. As for her schoolteachers, she's in a gay support group and they meet after PE.

Marnie is obviously someone of importance in their little pack, all of them attracted to the damage they share and the pains they've known. Urban living has certainly hardened them. The neglect and the poverty, it steals so much from children, forcing them to snatch whatever's offered them—and how they grab at the things put upon them by strangers, the unnatural comforts and abhorrent cruelties.

I'd like to take Marnie and Nelly far from here, but they don't even own a passport, it's like they're stuck on this irascible road until Marnie turns sixteen, but then what? A legal entitlement to a life on welfare. It's not to be leaned on, nor aspired to, there is more to them than that and if God grants me the time to make amends for an unfortunate boy set upon by me, I hope to show them.

Nelly

I curl up in a ball and scream. Mr. Domble doesn't know what to do with me and fetches the nurse. I silently fold the agony inside. They fetch Marnie. I grab for her, pulling at her shoulders, stretching at her V-neck. She grabs for my hands and pushes them away. She tells me to calm down. I feel a sop and a baby. I try to forget about them in the garden, really I do, but I can't, they live always in my head and so vividly. I see Izzy over Marnie's shoulder and I see Gene. I want to scream, but Marnie's eyes forbid it. She pulls me to my feet and we are allowed to go home.

"Lennie is asking questions," I tell her.

She ignores me and it fills me with fear.

"Lennie wishes to know their whereabouts," I persist. "But how can I tell him when he is teaching me Chopin?"

"You keep throwing fits like that then everyone is going to find out," she barks.

Our life is a calamity and I feel so damn angry these days. Perhaps on account of the things that cannot be ignored, deeds forced upon me by others. Oh damn Marnie, damn her to hell with her temper. I am thoroughly pained.

Marnie

She'd had a fit in the library and I had to take her home. She looked a right tit. She almost pulled my jersey off. I lifted her from the floor and nervously wiped her dress down. It was dusty. Mrs. MacLeod let us leave early.

Walking out of the school I held her hand. I couldn't help it. I hate her when she's like this but I feel other things too. She was shaking like a leaf and deep down I wanted to hug it all away, but the very thought made me feel uncomfortable and I was shamed by it.

When I look up at the voices yelling from the school windows and I see Nelly's classmates and they're shouting out "Freak" and "Weirdo," I am full of rage. I try to remember faces and plan to beat the offenders to a pulp. She is my sister and they have no right. When we get to Lennie's house I put her on the sofa. I tell Lennie she's had a fit at school. I explain to him she is prone to fits and he just accepts it, not a single question from him and I am so grateful. It's exhausting reaching for answers all the time. Nelly falls asleep and I go back to school. It feels safer there. I can't deal with her when she's like this, and when she wakes up I know I'll have nothing to say to her. It's like that right now.

Lennie

Nelly bled all over the sofa. Thank God I had the plastic covering over it. Marnie had gone back to school and so I had to get the tampons on my own. I thought of going to the chemist, but they know me in there and so I went to the supermarket and hid them under a box of cornflakes. Once Nelly had calmed down, and realized she wasn't going to drop dead, she was like a bloody budgie. Why was she bleeding? Why did her tummy hurt? How long does it last? I could have screamed. How the hell did she get to twelve, almost thirteen and not know any of this? My sisters couldn't wait to grow up, stuffing tissue down their bras at eleven years old and utterly jubilant when the bleeding came. I gave Nelly the tampons when I got back but it was obvious she didn't know how to use them. I didn't know what to say. I don't know how to use them either and so I made her some Ovaltine and gave her a chocolate digestive.

Of course the hardest part was having to tell her about cocks and vaginas, obviously I didn't use those particular words, but when it came to STDs and abortions I got straight to the point, especially for a girl blooming so rapidly and so beautifully. I suppose I didn't have to tell her about abortions, but in my thinking the sooner she knows about the consequences of premarital sex the better. Perhaps I should speak to Marnie about cocks and vaginas too, what a lady should and shouldn't be doing with them. She doesn't know either.

Marnie

I couldn't find it. Izzy made it. A photo album. She'd found all our family pictures, what there was of them and fixed them into a black binder with glue and sticky tape. I remember her putting it together, like a scrapbook. She kept waving baby snaps at me. There was one picture in particular taken in a park. Nelly was maybe a year old. Izzy was holding her close to her chest and Nelly was laughing and pointing at something in the distance. I was sort of pulling away from them and trying to run toward whatever Nelly was looking at beyond the camera, a slide we wanted to slip down maybe or a swing we wanted to play on. Gene was holding the camera.

I had a vague memory of this photo being in Izzy's hand, I remember Izzy drinking tea over it and looking sad, as if she didn't want to see it, but couldn't help looking at it. There was something about that picture and when I came into the room she hid it.

Their room was freezing. We had kept their bedroom window open to rid ourselves of Gene's smell and never closed it. Once inside I hugged myself, it was Baltic. In my head I kept seeing them, I could almost feel them, and I knew they weren't there, but I couldn't help thinking of them in the room. I remembered Gene sitting up in bed smoking a fag and holding a paper. He was watching Izzy from the corner of his eye changing out of jeans and into skirts, out of trainers and into shoes, attaching bobbles to her hair and spraying perfume on her wrists. And Nelly, next to Gene, a father and daughter side by side reading and that's all. Gene reaching for a mug of tea and slurping it dry. Nelly nibbling at a biscuit and letting the crumbs fall between the pages of her book. I'm at the end of the bed, picking at a scab formed after a fall. Izzy gives me shit for it, but I tell her to *fuck off*, it's just a knee. It feels like a loving time, a better time and it should comfort me, but it doesn't, it makes me ill inside and queasy. I pull back to the chill of the room and to their cast-iron frame, a rusting skeleton where they'd once slept, their mattress gone and dumped in the nighttime, a festering stain inking its fabric. We burned it a few days later in a nearby alleyway.

Izzy's photo album is by the bed and it makes me wonder if she'd fallen asleep with it in her hands and let it slip to the floor while looking at baby pictures of her children and photos of her mother or maybe the picture of Nelly and me playing in the grass in matching raincoats. I wonder if the album made her mostly happy or mostly sad, pictures are like that and will say anything you want them to, no one keeps the ones that don't.

The photo album is black and Izzy has written all of our names and birthdays on the inside, she's written her mother's name and her mother's birthday, her mother's death. She leaned heavy on the pen and didn't want to make a mistake. She didn't want to scribble, she wanted to be neat, as if her ink had a higher purpose.

The first few pictures in the album are of Izzy as a baby, impossible to imagine, but there she is in faded colors, a bonnet on her head, sitting upright in a Silver Cross pram. I find another, Izzy's two years old perhaps and in the arms of her mother, my grandmother, a petite brunette with poker-straight hair. She has the greenest eyes you've ever seen, like my eyes, only brighter. She dusts them in lavender and lines them in black. She's wearing a green miniskirt and an orange polo neck, a pair of platform shoes so thick and chunky they make her ankles look like little marbles.

Izzy's entire childhood is chronicled in just eight photographs, but there must have been others. Pictures of her father perhaps, but they're gone. Binned. Burned. Banished.

The last picture I come across was taken days before her mother died. Izzy sits by her mother, whose face is drawn and yellow, thinned by cancer and narrowed by a grin forced upon her by the camera. Izzy is also smiling, her long arm reaching across her mother's bed, holding her hand. It's a gentle pose, a farewell, the kind people take at train stations and airports, except it's not, Izzy's mother is dying and has days to live, and they will never see each other again. The next snap is Izzy several months later, heavily pregnant with me and committed to Eugene Doyle, he has a tin of beer in one of his hands and Izzy in the other.

It's in the middle of the album I find the picture I'm looking for. I can see boats in the background and a field surrounded by a stone wall. I know it's a park because there's a moss-colored climbing frame behind us. It's a bright day, a good day and the sun is shining and the weather is pure. I have no memory of it, all I have is this picture, a picture of happiness, and yet Izzy was frowning when she looked upon it. Was it regret? Hate? Did Izzy hate us I wondered?

I don't know why I vomited and why I felt warm and sticky with fear. Why I drank vodka with chocolate milk and crackers. Why I feel ashamed all the time. Why I miss them, the foulest of demons, my parents unkind and selfish. I don't even know why I'm sad or why I take the photo from the album and fold it into my back pocket or why my heart feels broken for an absent mother and an absent father. That's when I get it, I'm crying for what should have been. It's not a picture of a family in my back pocket, it's a picture of something she never really wanted. We were something that happened to her and though she held our hands and kissed our foreheads and sometimes tucked us into our beds, there was always a beat in her eyes as if she was thinking *What am I doing here?* and I know this because of the things she let happen to us.

I was alone in the house and could hear Nelly playing the violin, the same piece of music over and over again, it's crazy how quick she is to possess the things she's drawn to, how she absorbs her fascinations and wrings them dry. I love the violin, honestly I do, the way it dances with her entire being, but not on this day, on this day I want to burst through the wall and grab her by her scrawny neck, to choke her, anything to end the incessant playing of Bach and his dreary sonatas, to cease the sound of her bow buzzing like a wasp at my ear.

It was murder having to show her how to use a tampon. She was terrified and didn't understand. I say, "Do you want me to show you?" She nods. I lift my leg onto the toilet and tell her to "glide it into the vaginal canal." She totally freaks out, calls me a disgusting pig, starts hitting her head and the next thing she's pulling at the toilet roll on the wall and wrapping it around her hand until it forms a sort of tissue snowball. She stuffs it inside her pants and pulls up her knickers. She could hardly walk. I hate it when she's like this. I told her, "It won't stay like that. It will fall out." She kept shaking her head. There's no talking to her when she's like this. I bought her pads in the end. She took them and sulked of course, like it's my fault Izzy isn't here to show her.

Nelly

A white syringe. The coarsest cotton. It's abominable. I am bleeding a warmth so tight I feel hardened in my stomach. Every month they say. Every blasted month. Let the blood melt and be done with it I say. Marnie says it's unhygienic.

They talked of such ugly things and I am quite ill about it all. Boys and babies, they said, things our mother fell foul to, they said.

I must wear grown-up things now, says Marnie, all the while using words like *responsibility* and *maturity*. I am responsible. I am mature.

"Are they sensitive?" she asks.

"Whatever are you blabbing about?" I exclaim.

"Your breasts. That's how you'll know next month. Mine are always sensitive. Fucking agony sometimes," she tells me.

I can hardly find the words. What a thing to say and to her own sister. She says a great many things on this day, so does Lennie, but I am deaf to them both. I am deaf to it all.

It is disgusting to me.

Marnie

Kimbo's gay and proud these days and getting all this special treatment from everyone, especially at school, even Lennie lent an ear. Everyone is totally out to support her, except her mum, who's having a freak-out. Apparently she was upset she'd never have grandchildren until Kimbo reminded her she still has a womb. It's been hard for Kimbo. Her mum and dad are so embarrassed. Recently she accused them of ignoring her since she was born. Her mum went nuts at that, I mean Kimbo's parents let her do whatever she wants, but Kimbo says they only let her do what she wants because it's easier than not letting her do what she wants. I suppose she's right. They let her smoke at eleven and stay out past ten most weekends. She accused them of not being cool. They were gutted. She told them they exploited the idea of hip parenting to disguise neglect. Truth is her mum and dad are the only species on the planet surprised by Kimbo's sexual revelation. She's always been a butch girl and very aggressive, a bit of a bully to be honest. She says she beat women to hide her attraction to them. Now she's all sorry about it and apologizing to people like Sarah Pitt, a midget with bad hair. Anyway Kimbo kicked the crap out of her last year and got suspended for a week. Recently they had this mediation thing, organized by Mrs. MacLeod, who else. Anyway Kimbo asked Sarah to forgive her and Sarah complied, no one is going to debate with a sixteen-stone psychotic teenager. Now Kimbo's turning into a mediation addict and she's thumped a lot of people in her time, that's a lot of talking and a lot of hugging. Mrs. MacLeod is all over it.

Kimbo's so raw with emotion right now and likes to show her flesh, but only to draw attention to her piercings and of course the new tattoo, which I totally hate. It's her name. In Chinese. She doesn't even know anyone Chinese. And that's another thing, she doesn't want to be called Kimbo anymore. She said it's a name we gave to her because we needed to define the masculine in her without dealing with what the masculine in her actually meant, in other words her being a lemon. She said Kim is a woman who loves women and Kimbo was a woman who hated herself, so now we call her Kim. She said we're not to stereotype her. It's her favorite word these days. She also likes the word *cliché*.

It's been such a long week and I'm exhausted. Kim keeps going on about me getting a tattoo, but I don't want one. For a start it looks sore. Susie got one, of course she did. No willpower that one. A ring of ivy around her ankle for her mum. I just don't get why anyone would want to ink their name or their secrets on the surface of their skin, why can't they just keep them inside like I do? I saw this girl at the Barras last summer. Tall. Blond. Dreadlocks, about thirty years old and she was like a human drawing. Not kidding. Head to toe in tattoos, it felt like her entire body was screaming at me.

I'm never getting a tattoo. My secrets are etched safely on the inside and I intend to keep them there.

Nelly

They laughed at me and then they were angry.

"You can't wear your used PE things under your school uniform," Sharon growled. "It's disgusting. Unhygienic. You need to take them off and have a shower like a normal person."

"I will do as I jolly well please," I retorted.

She grabbed me by the lapels.

"Take off your fucking clothes or I'll take them off for you," she spat.

"No," I whispered.

And so she grabbed me. Attempted to undress me and so I punched the air and twisted and turned. I would not make it easy for her.

"She's like a fucking fish." Sharon laughed. They all laughed.

"Someone hold her down!" she yelled.

They stripped me to the bone and before I could say Jiminy Cricket I was under the shower and soaped to the core.

"Someone get her a towel!" yelled Sharon.

I was still screaming, or was I crying? It's all a blur now.

"Dry yourself," commanded Sharon.

I knew better than to disobey and so I dried myself.

"If you ever come to this changing room after PE and not

shower before you leave or wear your clothes under your uniform again I will fucking have you. Understand? Dirty cow."

I nodded and from that day forward I made sure I was only wearing my vest and my knickers beneath my uniform and when I left I was sure to shower. Everything was tickety boo after that, though I was advised to wear a bra by Marnie.

"I'll do no such thing," I told her.

"Fine. Don't wear a bra. Get your head kicked in by Sharon and don't wear a bra. I don't care," Marnie says.

"Talk to her, Marnie. She'll listen to you."

"I don't want her to listen to me. I want you to listen to her and I want you to listen to me. Wear a fucking bra. Take one of mine."

I went to Marnie's drawers. She had all kinds of paraphernalia in there, laces and satins. Reds and blues, pinks and yellows. I chose a white one and a black.

"That's great, Nelly," said Marnie and in an approving tone. She fitted them to my body and I wanted to cry.

"I can't," I said, trying to struggle out of them.

"They'll sag if you don't," she said. "It'll stop them jumping about, it'll stop the boys staring at them if you wear the right one." I eventually found the right one.

"That's good, Nelly. You look good."

The following week when I go to gym wearing my bra Sharon whistles at me, my face reddens and I want to get dressed again.

"Suits you," says Sharon. "You've a nice wee bod." The girls in the changing room agree and we go to PE. My body feels comfortable in the bra and I find it easier to jump at the basketball hoops. It hurts less.

Afterward I take a shower. Sharon nods in approval.

She was being nice to me in the changing room, but still, I made sure to keep all contact with Sharon Henry to an absolute minimum after that, she is a rough girl devoid of manners and always giggling with the boys. I don't know how they stand her.

Marnie

I got there late. I had to walk and didn't have the fare for the bus, also I wanted Kirkland to think I wasn't coming. I don't want to lead him on. He's an all-right guy, I suppose, but I don't fancy him and he needs to know that so I don't exactly burst my hole trying to get there, also I got lost and couldn't find his house. I had to walk up every set of stairs I passed along the street, looking at names on doors. One tenement had twelve names on the buzzer. Eventually I find the name Milligan engraved on an ornate gold plate and I'm about to rap the door when I see this giant fuck-off door knocker. Honest to God, I could hardly lift the thing, so I try knocking with my knuckles but the door's solid and it hurts. I was getting totally fed up hanging around in the freezing cold and that's when I decide to give it a kick and get myself heard and I did it a couple of times until the door swings opens and there's Kirkland totally delighted to see me, but then he's looking right past me and saying, "Where have you been?" Behind me a woman's voice says, "Supermarket." I turn round to see who he's talking to and there's this thirtysomething couple getting out of a Volkswagen Beetle. I could have died.

"Want a hand?" says Kirkland to Mummy.

"Sure," says Mummy to Kirkland.

I follow suit.

"Can I help?" says Marnie to Daddy.

"I think we've got it," says Daddy to Marnie.

Their car had been sitting there the whole time and they'd seen me kicking the arse out of their front door.

Within a few minutes it's clear they think I'm Kirkland's girlfriend and even clearer they're not happy about it. I want to correct them and make them feel better by telling them I wouldn't touch Kirkland with a shitty stick, but I feel so bad about kicking in the door I don't say anything.

They're a good-looking couple and quite young. His mum tells me to call her Fiona and his dad says his name is Gus. She's posh and he's not, but they obviously have money. Turns out she's a journalist and he writes crap television.

They stay frosty for a while, but they know they need to melt for Kirkland's sake and of course they have a million questions to ask.

First question.

"So, what school do you go to, Marnie?"

The rudest question you'll ever be asked in Glasgow, along with "Where do you live?" 'cause saying Maryhill is way too vague. Believe it or not there are nice parts of Maryhill, but I don't live in those parts. Should be enough to just say Maryhill but it won't be, my answer will permit or negate the judgment they've already bestowed upon me. I decide to get my own back, let them sweat it.

I move closer to Kirkland and decide to act like I am his girlfriend and put my hand next to his hand, touching him barely but enough to get the effect I need from Mr. and Mrs. Not So Liberal as They Like to Think. Then I go in for the kill.

"I live in Sighthill, Gus, but I'm currently attending Mary-hill Academy."

"That's quite a trek," he says.

"It's a good school," I say. "That's important, no?"

Obviously I don't live in Sighthill, I just want to rattle his cage a wee bit and as expected something flickers across both their faces.

Now for a question he won't ask.

How the fuck did my son meet a slag from Sighthill?

Some questions she won't ask.

Are you a drug addict? A whore?

The tension in the room is well tasty unlike the green tea they're serving in this tiny wee teapot with matching egg cups. They're dying for me to ask about it so they can babble about their halcyon days living in Tibet. Five minutes in the room and these people are seriously giving me the dry boke; so is their fucking tea.

To ease the atmosphere Kirkland tells them I go to school with Lorna. Fiona likes Lorna. Feels safe with her name in the room, even calls her talented. Apparently Lorna plays guitar. They love that shit, and we start talking about the enrichment programs at Maryhill. Susie's doing that program, the drama one. Then they bitch about Lorna's Conservative parents but only to illuminate how *right on* they think they are. Next thing they're on at Kirkland about being a doctor and going to Africa and that throws me 'cause I didn't know he wanted to go into medicine or go to Africa. Then Kirkland goes, "I told you, I don't want to be a doctor."

Fiona says, "Course you do."

Kirkland says, "Naw I don't."

"Don't say naw to your maw, it's no," says Gus.

"I'm just saying I'm not going to be a doctor."

"You used to want to be a doctor," says Fiona.

"Do you want him to be a doctor?" I ask.

Fiona gives me the dirtiest look I've ever seen, then she says, "Kirkland's been very blessed in life. We all have. It's important to give back to the world. It's what we believe. We're Buddhists."

I'm not remotely thrown by that, of course they're Buddhists. I look around, and sure enough there's the bronze fat guy where a fireplace used to be. Wee water feature nearby.

"So, you think he can save the world or something?" I say.

"Kirkland can do anything he sets his mind to," nips Gus.

"Doesn't have to be the third world or anything, you don't even have to be a doctor, just make a contribution to the Universe, develop a world beyond your own, son. Engineering, perhaps."

"I'll give it some thought," says Kirkland, who won't give it any thought and not 'cause he doesn't care but because they're telling him who to be and no one knows that at sixteen.

"What about you, Marnie? Do you have plans for the future?"

"Hairdressing," I say. "But not in the third world. Maybe Byres Road." Obviously they expected nothing less and who am I to disappoint. Anyway, telling them I want to be a lawyer would please them, make them all comfy and they don't deserve it.

I reach for the tiny teapot, not 'cause I like their rotten tea but because I've already worked out Fiona is totally anal and the action of helping myself, even though I've been listening to them going on about the virtues of global sharing, makes Fiona nervous.

"Let me get that for you," she says. I make a big show of drinking it and make lots of yummy slurping sounds, like my whole life will change because my tea is green.

Eventually they get off their arses and make me lunch. Paninis. Everything vegetarian and organic of course. Must have cost a fortune. I want to reject the food just to piss them off, but I don't. I'm starvin' like Marvin. Then they start going on about cancer and how organic living is the way forward, totally ignoring how expensive it is to be organic and that there are a lot of people out there grateful if they can afford regular living. I can hardly swallow.

Dessert is served with coffee, except it's not coffee, it's espresso and like their daft tea it's served in egg cups. I decide to get Kirkland a huge fuck-off mug for Christmas to dwarf all these tiny wee dishes his mum's got. Fiona gives me a huge slice of cake, but remains unable to mask her discomfort, basically she wants me to fuck off and never come back and is totally shiting it in case I drag her son off to Sighthill and start injecting him with heroin.

Out of nowhere Gus announces he's from Sighthill. He doesn't elaborate or anything but he's obviously embarrassed. I don't ask too many questions though I'm dying to know how someone from Sighthill ends up in a town house in Kelvinside, while Gus is wondering how a girl from Sighthill ended up in his designer kitchen.

"Meeting Fiona saved my life." He puts his hand on her hand, she cooperates but she really wants him to shut the fuck up about their business so she changes the subject pronto.

"So, Marnie, what does your father do?"

"He's a stockbroker at LGL, Fiona."

"Really," she says.

"Naw. He's an alkie, left when I was wee."

The room freezes. I want to laugh so hard, I mean it's mostly true, except he's not going anywhere, not in the state he's in.

"Sorry to hear that, Marnie," says Gus.

"Marn," I correct even though it's not what I'm called and it doesn't have any ring to it.

"Right, Marn." He doesn't think it has a ring to it either.

Then Gus says, "I know what you're going through, what it's like to live with people like that."

He's totally softened, Fiona just about disappears up her own arse when he confides this.

"My da was a drinker, but then he stopped. Came back into my life and tried to make amends for the things he'd done, you know, but it was too late. He died last year," he says.

"And your mum?" I ask.

"Cancer," he says. "Been gone ten years now."

I want to say I'm sorry but I don't get a chance. Fiona says, "More coffee?" to indicate the end of lunch and my imminent departure.

"I'm fine. Not really into espresso," I say.

"Let's go, Marn!" says Kirkland, emphatic on the Marn.

"Nice meeting you," I say to Gus and Fiona, but to be honest it was only nice meeting Gus, now that I've got to know him and all that.

Before I leave we go to Kirkland's room to get my coat, but really to sell Kirkland two jellies courtesy of Mick. Kirkland loves jellies. Now I know why.

Lennie

His name's Robert Macdonald and he abandoned his wife and his daughter. He tells me that he was an alcoholic and of his shame for beating Isabel and her mother. I don't know what to make of it all. He tells us Isabel was ten years old when he left her. He talks of his regrets and his need to say sorry to a woman who has in fact abandoned her own children. He says he's been looking for Isabel for a long time. Robert T. Macdonald is a craftsman now and looking to make amends. He makes rocking chairs and sells them on the Internet, to Americans mostly. He wants to impress Nelly by how changed he is, but Nelly seems afraid of such assertions and not sure what they mean from someone who is nothing more than a stranger.

He possesses an incautious honesty and I can't deny I'm intrigued by the eyes belonging to the younger of his grandchildren. I tell him Isabel and Gene are in Turkey. We just want him to go away. I tell him I'm closely acquainted with his daughter and assure him she won't be back until September, I say she's an artist and paints landscapes. He likes this story, as does Nelly. It makes him relieved in a way, lessens his remorse slightly for a life he imagines went on in spite of him and not because of him. If only that were true. At that moment I want to tell him the truth, he deserves it. *Your whore daughter could be anywhere.* Obviously I don't say that. He's a very big man. Hands like shovels.

When he leaves he thanks me for the tea and the lemon loaf I baked the night before. Personally I thought it was a little dry, but he had two slices, which was very good of him. Anyway he hands me a picture of his child and immediately I am struck by how like Marnie she is. Robert asks me to give Isabel the picture, it has a number inked on the back, an old snap, faded in places, and a much younger man I suppose to be him holding tight a child I know to be Isabel. The picture leaves Nelly shaken. She grabs it and won't let it go. He sees this and our eyes lock. This is when Marnie arrives, just flings open the door and there she is, soaked to the bone.

"Isabel," he says.

Nelly

A graying fellow who said he was our grandfather, the father of our mother.

Lennie was a gentleman as always, able to ignore his admissions of violence but I was frightened by them.

We must lie to the chap, this much I am sure of. Telling the truth doesn't matter to a stranger for he knows little and can judge nothing.

Mother has gone and there is nothing to be done and the man who eats practically *all* of Lennie's cake must leave and before Marnie returns for she will positively faint at the sight of him.

Marnie

He says he was in Barcelona, Seville, Morocco, and Egypt. He seeks out carpentry designs from other lands. Furniture. Talks about chairs for a while. I want to douse myself in petrol and light a fag. He's boring. Very boring. Drones an entire life at me. I look at the photograph of Izzy as a child holding tight her father's hand and I want to throw something at him. I imagine the pain she'd feel looking at the picture, I imagine her recalling a life beyond the photograph, and I imagine her heartbreak. She told us how he beat her, how he beat her mother and though he's sorry for his sins it's too late to atone for them, except he doesn't know that and I do, so does Nelly. It's pathetic and sad, but not for him. For his daughter, dead and not quite buried. I want to drink and smoke and feel like I can't. I just want him to leave and there's Lennie passing out cups and saucers, lighters and ashtrays. I decide fuck it and pull out a cigarette, see what Grandpa will do and he flinches a little, I offer him one but he refuses, says he stopped when he found Jesus.

I smoke my cigarettes, staring into his eyes, it feels like we're cowboys on a dusty trail sizing each other up before we shoot each other. My gun is loaded. I don't have to check, the bullet is a dead daughter. I don't know what his bullet is.

"She told us you were dead."

"Well I'm not," he says.

"Obviously," I say back.

"This cake is divine Lennie, truly it is," says Nelly, lightening the atmosphere except she doesn't. "You're quite the chef, old man. Isn't he a find, Mr. Macdonald?"

He doesn't say anything for a minute, like everyone else who meets Nelly for the first time, he's stunned and silent. Absorbing, not comprehending. He nods.

"It's fantastic," he tells Lennie.

Nelly smiles at me, a knowing look in her eye. We will never tell this stranger where Izzy is. We are keeping our secret and we are keeping it from everyone.

Lennie

When the girls woke up and found him on the sofa they weren't best pleased and when I say "they" I mean Marnie, but it's my house and I can invite who I like. Anyway he was sickly and almost passed out on the floor at the sight of her. She is so like Isabel as a child it frightened him half to death and rather surprised me for they look nothing like one another, not now. We spent the evening talking is all. I needed to get the measure of him. Protect them. He's not all there. I can see it in his eyes.

First thing I do is the politics conversation. He's a staunch Conservative and very religious. Then he starts a conversation about his travels, obviously he thought it would fascinate me, but I've done some traveling in my own life and wasn't too impressed. I found him broken in places, hidden places. I found him dull.

He makes quite a bit of money doing what he does and was very candid about his earnings. He plans to offer much of it to his lost daughter and probably thinks it will make a difference, perhaps change her, but it won't and anyway it's not that kind of money. He'll definitely be comfortable, be able to keep a house and live out his years. He has a stall at the Barrowland, a busy workshop, and an apprentice he's proud of, a young lad he found on the streets, he says. He pays him a small wage for minding the stall and is teaching him the trade. The lad lives in Robert's workshop. Robert says he's a born carpenter. It's a marvelous thing to have done for a child and this I was impressed by, but the rest of him? I suppose he's amiable enough, but there's an edge to the man, I can feel it, something sour and it's vexing. He says he has a Web site and calls himself the Tartan Craftsman. The Americans flock to him, but he'll need more than a catchy title to get the attentions of his grandchildren, that much I do know.

He's obviously interested in the girls, though he certainly wasn't prepared for Nelly, and you could see Marnie's smoking rattled his cage. Of course he wants to know all about Isabel, but I don't have a great deal to tell him about his daughter and what I do know he won't want to hear. He is full of remorse and shame and told me stories of her mother, his ex-wife, which filled me with pity for the girl, but then an image of Izzy in a shopping trolley, legs akimbo, swilling back the Buckfast emerged and my sympathy was somewhat diluted.

He asked if I thought she might be looking for him. I shook my head. I felt sorry for him then. He sort of shrugged it off as a joke, but I know he meant it.

Breakfast was a big affair. It always is in my house: sausages, bacon, fried bread and egg (I'm trying desperately to fatten up Marnie at the moment, skin and bones that one). I think she's anorexic. I asked her if she was feeling okay the other day and of course she says she's fine, then she grabs a piece of toast and she's out the door faster than a fly.

They stay here mostly. They sneak in through the back, so the neighbors don't see, not that the neighbors see a great deal, blind to most things in fact, including the absence of two abhorrent parents and the abandonment of two lost children. I feel quite sick about it. Who wouldn't?

Marnie

Lennie let Izzy's dad stay over. I nearly died when I saw him on the sofa. Asked me what was I up to today? I said, "Nothing," and ran out the door before he started asking more questions.

What's he doing here? What does he want? He's got some neck on him that's for sure, thinking he can just show up like this. And what exactly does he expect? That Izzy's going to turn up and fall into his arms? She probably would, knowing her, if she actually had any arms. She was like that, a total people pleaser, she couldn't say no to anyone, including Gene.

He keeps asking us if we need anything but I'd rather eat shite than take his money. It seems to me if he'd been a better father we might have had a better mother.

Now he's going to hang about and wait for her and when she doesn't turn up he'll ask more questions. It's a mess. The one thing making it easier to hide Gene and Izzy in the flower beds is the fact no one except Mick is interested in their whereabouts. It turns out Gene was selling for him and when he "left," Gene owed Mick a lot of money. Mick says it's worth thousands, but it's thousands he owes to Vlado and like his associates Vlado doesn't give a flying fuck why Mick can't pay so Mick had to sell half the stuff in his house including a very nice flat-screen television, but it still wasn't enough. Vlado actually came to the van the other night. I was doing some revision in the back. He just takes the book off me and flicks through the pages and then he asks me if I know the difference between the perimeter of a circle and the circumference of a circle.

I said, "The circumference of a circle is the length of the curve that surrounds it."

"And how is this exemplified?"

"By its center and its radius."

"What is the ratio of the circumference of a circle to its diameter?"

I say, "Pi."

"Very good," he says and returns the book to me. Then he looks me up and down like he did in the stairwell and says, "It is better to study. No?"

"I suppose."

He makes no reply, as if he'd spoken to himself, as if I hadn't spoken at all.

When Mick got back from the tower, Vlado pulls him to the side. Vlado's taller than Mick, younger, stronger. His face is hard, his eyes soft. His hair is dark and fine and falls a little over his face. He wears a short army coat. Leather boots. Smells clean, as if he just had a shower.

Anyway I could tell they were talking about me, all the time looking back at me and nodding, a few pulled faces, Vlado's finger prodding at Mick's shoulder, pushing him a little, don't know what they were saying, but Mick looked scared. When he gets back to the van I asked him what Vlado's problem was and Mick says, "He doesn't want you working with me anymore."

"What's it got to do with him?" I ask.

"Everything," he says.

"So that's it? No more rounds."

"No more rounds," he says.

"So he's making you fire me?"

"I'm sorry."

"But I need the money!"

"I don't give a shit what you need. Your da's got ma money and see when I find him I'm going to rip his fucking throat out."

"What about us?"

"You're fifteen. I'm married. S'over."

I don't even know what to say to that. He parks the van for a minute.

"If Gene shows up call me, if he shows up and you don't call me, you'll know about it, hen. Understand?"

"You owe me money," I say.

"And when your da gives me mine, I'll give you yours." Then he drives off. I'm not even near my house, only three quid on me and it's late. I want to kill that Vlado. It's none of his business how I earn, but Mick's terrified of Vlado and terrified of the people he works for. Dangerous people. It serves him right for getting greedy. Gene had connections at the colleges and universities and Mick said they were making good money, until Gene went missing that is.

Don't know where he put it, the stash I mean. I know it's not in the house, but it might be and so every day before school I check a new corner, but nothing.

It's been a shit week all round to be honest. Nelly forgot her own birthday and got upset when we remembered. Lennie baked her a cake and Nelly threw it at the wall. Seriously. Then she started crying and then screaming. It was a total scene. Lennie was horrified. He'd gotten her a nice box of perfume and I got her earrings but then I decided to keep them on account of her being a nightmare bitch. I was glad when she went to her room. So was Lennie. She's such a weirdo freak sometimes. I hate saying it but it's true. Why can't she be normal?

Later on I went to Kirkland's house and we shagged, I don't know why. After we're done, he wants to smooch but I just want to get away from him. I feel sick we had sex to be honest. He tries to give me money for a taxi home and that makes me feel like a prostitute so I says, "Fuck off. I'll walk." He goes all mortified then and offers to come with me, I tell him it's only nine o'clock and rapists don't start work till after the pubs close. He thinks that's funny 'cause he's an idiot. Then he lets me go and tries to give me a kiss, but I don't let him. I don't even like him.

Nelly

How I raged at Lennie for his teenage cake, at Marnie for her teenage gift. What need have I for earrings? I have no piercings. It's not a special day, it has never been a special day, and I am not different on account of it. Why couldn't they forget as I had? Cakes and gifts. Candles and icing. Thirteen years of age it said. Happy Birthday it said. How dare they. Intolerable. Infuriating. I won't hear of it. It is not my birthday. It has never been my birthday or perhaps Marnie has forgotten the waiting for Mother and Father to recall such days. The wide-open mouths when they are reminded, the shame of having to remind them at all. Maybe Marnie has forgotten her own thirteenth year when Father called her a woman and followed her from room to room with daisies and gin. I have not forgotten for it is flawed to offer a teenager alcohol. It is forbidden. One can get into a great deal of trouble with the law for enticing a minor. Fortunately she didn't drink any, but he did and a great deal if memory serves. Mother had fallen asleep and didn't seem to care at all that evening, not even for Marnie, who was forced to like daisies, a flower she doesn't care for at all.

Lennie

Nelly was furious, which is a shame because I'd made her a beautiful birthday cake, a raspberry sponge filled with butter cream and a stunning liqueur sauce. I could have screamed when she threw it at the wall. She could have at least tasted it first. What a child she is and crying all over the place while I'm wondering how to get the bloody cake off the wall-paper. She needed her arse whipped for that. I can just imagine my mother's face if I'd thrown as much as a teaspoon in our house. Very strict my mother was and as for my father he spent most of my life on a chair by the window reading his news-papers and cleaning his glasses. I don't think he looked up at me for thirty-five years and even when he did, it was only be-cause he'd fallen on his arse and needed help to a chair.

"Good job, Lennie," he said.

When my mother died he was suddenly all alone in the house, but would he leave it? No he wouldn't.

"It's my home and I intend to stay in it, I will not languish in a hospital bed. I'd rather die behind the door," he yelled and that's exactly what happened. He'd called my sister Eve and said he was feeling poorly and could she come round, but Eve wouldn't go and so the cheeky bitch called me. He'd had a stroke and his little body was so cold I couldn't exactly say how long he'd lain there, but not long, old people are always cold aren't they? Still, I felt bad and for a long time afterward. Even now I wonder if I could have gotten there quicker but I was in the middle of dinner wasn't I? I didn't know he was going to die.

I often wonder where I would like to die. I'm an old man and I've been ailing of late. The doctor says I need an MRI and would like to rule out a few variables. I suppose it wouldn't hurt.

I feel very anxious at the moment, I don't quite know why, especially for my dog . . . oh . . . I feel anxious at the moment and for the dog . . . anxious. And dog. I feel anxious for the dog. I am anxious for the dog.

Nelly

Robert T. Macdonald hasn't mentioned my birthday. He doesn't know and I am glad of it. There is no cake and there are no candles. There is eggs and there is bacon. Food of the proletariat. There are also potato scones but I don't care for any of it. I only eat what I eat.

He slurps his tea like a navvy, I observe. He offers beans. He offers cola in a glass. There are no cornflakes.

"I need cereal," I announce.

He tells the waitress. She nods and brings me a bite-size box of Krispies.

"No," I gasp in horror. "I need cornflakes. Cornflakes. Please. I can't eat these. I want cornflakes."

"It's okay. Calm down. We'll get you cornflakes," he assures me.

His voice is gentle and I feel quite calmed.

The waitress is quick to return.

"Can you take these back?" he asks. "We need cornflakes over here."

"So I heard," she mocks. Awful woman. Jangling earrings and nails like Nosferatu himself. She is cheap and unwholesome.

Within minutes she returns with a similar-size box of what has to be the best of nourishment. I pour cola over a crisp and bubbling bowl.

"Taste good, does it?" He smiles.

I nod.

"Like nothing on earth," I tell him.

He asks questions, questions about Izzy, about Gene, but mostly about Lennie. I don't have any questions, not for Robert T. Macdonald, I only have answers, all of them lies. Lies are imperative these days. I don't tell him about our trip to the Loch either. It's not his business, nothing is his business.

Spring

Lennie

Verdurous glens and ochre risings, the long journey to Firemore. I made sandwiches for the trip. Ham and cheese. A flask of tea. I love tea. Cartons of Ribena and yogurts for the girls. Things kids like. Some pick and mix and chocolate bars, also jelly babies.

The girls are surprised I can drive. I have to rent a car of course, an SUV, a big car, lots of room and nothing like your precious Saab, how you loved that car. I begged you to get rid of it, but you wouldn't have it, even when the tire burst and we got stuck outside Inverness. Pissing with rain it was and no more bloody tea. It was freezing. This car wouldn't break down, it had a CD player and everything, Marnie was delighted. It even had these little headsets, like on an airplane and so Marnie could listen to what she liked.

I could see the girls in the rearview mirror. Marnie bobbing her head rhythmically and Nelly drawing smiley faces on the window. She seemed happy enough, she read a bit and played Sudoku mostly. Every few hours we had to take the dog for a walk but with the leash, just in case he ran off. Marnie was thrilled about that. I don't think she likes my dog.

It was a windy walk to the cottage. We parked the car next to the river stone wall, it's old now, falling apart at the seams, but still, we managed to climb over it and without too much fussing.

They were certainly awestruck by the cottage, of course I'm used to the sight of it, but watching them enjoy the landscape renewed my perspective somewhat and it seemed more picturesque than usual, especially with the sea bouncing about the beach like a happy dog.

When we got to the house it was freezing but there were plenty of logs in the shed, I had the place toasty in no time. Nelly and Marnie went down to the water and I made us some dinner.

Washing the potatoes I watched them through the window, it seems I'm always watching them, trying to glean a little information I suppose, but they're very quiet about the things missing in their lives. They were throwing stones and collecting shells, things children do when they're near water. I saw Marnie at the edge of the sands, the Loch rolling in and out. It made me a little nervous at first, I was worried she'd drift away, but she was just playing and soaked her socks. Nelly found herself a stick and drew love hearts in the sand. She wrote names on the inside, boys most likely. Marnie didn't like it too much and sat on her own and quite a distance from her. Nelly followed her and sat next to her and then she put her arms around her and gave her a hug. I shouldn't have spied that, it was a very private moment but I was frozen behind the pane. Then they went for a walk, hand in hand. Warm. Close. Impenetrable. The dog tottering behind them.

We had a lovely meal later and Nelly made a crumble and all on her own with apples and blackberries. She did a good job of it. She's been watching me in the kitchen recently, there was a little too much crumble for my liking to be honest, but we'll work on that. I showed her how to make lamb, nice leg with rosemary and a little garlic, and then we ate and talked some, like a real family.

Marnie confided her plan to go to university, though she's not too sure what she should study. She has a hard time imagining herself as anything other than the girl she is today.

They were very interested in the cottage and how we came to own it etc. I told them how you inherited it from Edward, your mother's obscure brother, the frightened poof from Somerset, not that it runs in families, but a blind man running for a bus could have told them he was queer, it should have been bloody obvious given he had no interest in women, choosing instead to live as a recluse. He was exiled as far as I'm concerned. It was only later that it occurred to us your family might have known all along, colluding with Edward to harbor him in this cottage, ashamed and hiding from who he really was. You certainly lived in terror of them ever finding out about you, but it was the same situation really, no girl of your own and living with your dear old chum Lennie from the college. A feigned ignorance if you want my opinion.

It was very sad rummaging through the loneliness he'd left behind. The vintage boxing posters of sweaty bare-chested men bruised and wearing mouth guards. The VHS collection that included a box set of *Phantom of the Opera* and a rather disturbing interest in the queen of England.

It was a tribute to him living here as we did, bringing an awaited solace to his retreat by the sea and with an honesty he never knew in life and a love he'd probably wished for a thousand times. We always felt divine in this place, tasting a desired view of the world, knowing a voracious appetite for the love that dare not speak its name, my soul sewn to your soul. Our fortunate embroidery.

Nelly

What a splendid trip. Fishing on a boat. Reading by the fire. Walking on the moors. We toasted marshmallows, enjoyed sardines on toast. I even slept with Bobby, I got very cold at the cottage. No central heating. As for Marnie and me, we mended our rift and I forgave her for the blow to my mouth. We're family and we must stick together through this trying time. Keep the parents buried and her secret safe. She really is the most wonderful sister. I am blessed and I am safe, though she didn't like what I wrote in the sand too much. My sister has a profound problem with one thinking for oneself and of course the thoughts that occupy my head are not always what she desires of me, but I cannot help how I feel and I cannot help the things I must say. Truth be known I keep much of my heart to myself and for the most part I remain silent. It is all she needs from me right now and in this respect she will always have my loyalty.

Marnie

I didn't want to go to be honest. A week with Nelly in a space I can't run from scared the shit out of me. As for Lennie, he's a great guy and we couldn't do without him right now, but he's a wee bit controlling these days and always telling me what to do. He says thing like "young lady" and loves the word *conscientious*. It gets on my tits to be honest. I know he's trying to help, but I don't need help. I need to be left alone. I've got exams in a couple of weeks. I'm not worried or anything, but still, it's stressful, all that scratching on paper. I always finish first, and then I have to hang about waiting for everyone else, they won't let you leave early. Sometimes I feel like not showing up and forcing a fail, sleeping in or something. I did that for a maths exam once. Mr. Weston was so pissed off. He called me "wasteful" and gave me lines, a hundred of them. Three pages of total bullshit, back and sides. What a tosser!

The trip up was nice, we had a cool car and I got to drown out Nelly with my headphones, although she didn't have too much to say for herself for a change. Also she just loves being anywhere Lennie is. Thinks he's family, her grandpa. I suppose she needs someone to care for her, I can't be arsed at the moment. She was so excited before we left, packed her bag three days before and read the whole trip, which was bliss.

His cottage was amazing, the kind of place you dream of

calling home, but it's so fucking far away and freezing, but still, a great place to hide out. It has its own beach and its own sea, you can't go wrong in a place like this. Nelly and I had a bit of a nip, she wrote Izzy's and Gene's names in a love heart on the sand and then RIP underneath. I made her rub it out and then I sulked on the sand in order to underline my displeasure. She was very sorry and I felt bad for her then, especially when she gave me a hug. I let her. She doesn't mean it, not really. She's just daft and I also didn't want to spoil our holiday. I knew it was going to be nice because of the Loch, it smelled great and calmed me down.

Lennie had a boat, full of surprises, that guy, he can row it and everything. He took us fishing, we didn't catch anything but then like magic we had trout for dinner. Lennie freezes everything. He has spaghetti sauce coming out his ears and loads of Tupperware filled with all kinds of other sauces, he brought it all up in one of those ice boxes, along with clams and scallops and bread, shortbread even. The guy would freeze his arm if he thought he could make a nice bourguignonne with it. He's so into cooking, the kind of person who makes appetizers. Waste of food if you ask me, fills you up and you can't eat your dinner but he likes to make them and I love the hummus. I could suck it with a straw. Lennie could quite literally hang about his kitchen for hours, no joke and don't get me started on the spice rack, he worships it. Has mad stuff in it like bay leaves and tarragon and you should see the oven he's got, it must be a hundred years old, fuck knows how they got it down here.

The other thing I love about Lennie is how he sets the table for dinner, you feel like you're in a fancy restaurant sometimes. He puts out a tablecloth with matching napkins and whatever seashells, pebbles, or flowers he's found that day, then he layers them in vases or arranges them on hand-painted plates, one time he got heather and tied it up with thread and put it lengthwise on this white wicker thing and then he added a few candles, some shells, it was fucking celestial. To be honest he's a bit of a people pleaser, he needs a lot of praise and a lot of approval, like a kid and it's really annoying 'cause if I'm doing something, homework, reading, or watching TV, he'll drag me away to look at shopping he's bought or clothes he's ironed or a pot of soup he's made, obviously he wants gratitude, but I don't know how to show it, I go through the motions obviously, make smiley faces and stuff, you know, to show my appreciation, but he wants more than that, a more concrete acknowledgment, a thank-you perhaps, but I just can't say it, makes me feel uncomfortable and I hate that feeling. Truth is I don't really know the word, it's a bit of a stranger in my vocabulary and it's not like I've had a reason to spit bullets of gratitude my whole life or have parents who gave me a reason to be thankful. Even when I was grateful it wasn't for the things a normal person would be grateful for:

"Thanks for not coming home with total strangers and keeping me up all night with 'Blue Monday'"; "Thanks for buying eggs and not crack this week"; "Thanks for making it to the toilet last night and not shitting all over the sofa"; and last, but not least, "Thanks for suffocating yourself, Izzy, and making it easier to move your dead body into a coal bunker."

See what I mean. Sentiment unknown. Sounds brutal I know, but what do you want, with my background I should be a serial killer. Count your blessings.

Still, wish I'd thanked Nelly for the amazing dinner she

made the other night. She's turning into quite the gourmet these days. She made us clams with tomato sauce. Lennie was so proud. We danced that night. I had a lot of fun.

I know I should be grateful for people like Lennie, he's been amazing to us and cares for us, but it scares me. I don't know why. Just does.

Lennie

It was our last day at the cottage. I didn't mean to talk ill of them. We were all so warm and safe together, like a family. I couldn't stop myself. We had walked a good way along the Loch to have a picnic. Nelly collected shells for a box she wants to make and I took some blankets, a hamper of food, the chicken I roasted in the morning, the bread I'd freshly baked the night before. We went to the sandy spot under the rock shaped like a leaf. The girls took their shoes and socks off and ran into the water, it was freezing out and I was worried they'd catch pneumonia, but who am I to stop the laughter of children. I'd brought tea in a flask and Irish coffee for me in the other, my special recipe. Anyway we got to talking about Mummy and Daddy and I got a little irate I suppose. I didn't say anything offensive, I just stated the facts. They're gone and they're probably not coming back. Marnie was furious. She suggested I wanted to keep her and Nelly to myself so I can play house, and asked me which one of them I liked best. I told her I liked them both the same, I told her not to worry and she always has a home as long as we're neighbors. She said I was getting old and couldn't promise such things and maybe I can't. I could see instantly she was very worried about the "monsters'" return and yet counting on them to come back. I told her it's pretty unlikely, but from her face I could see she was hurting, so I reminded her who her parents were and how they have treated Nelly and how they've treated her. Maybe the coffee went to my head a little, but when I think of those people leaving these children to their own devices, to survive in a cold and cruel world with not a word of their whereabouts and not a scrap of food in the house I want to hang them out to dry. They deserve better than that, these girls. They keep themselves clean, do well in school, and with those two menaces for parents it's a bloody miracle they're alive at all. Children deserve to be loved, and if you can't love them you shouldn't have them. Marnie went quite pale at these particular assertions, that's when I realized I'd hurt her. All things considered it obviously never occurred to me anyone could love such impossible things, how Marnie had loved them and how Nelly might have loved and perhaps had been loved in return, somewhere inside of them and somewhere forgotten. I wanted to say sorry but it didn't belong in the conversation.

Marnie went off on her own then. Nelly stayed and ate the rest of the chicken. Later I made a strudel, Marnie loves strudel and when she got back she smiled at me as if to say she was sorry, which I appreciated, but I could tell she'd been crying, I could tell she'd been breaking her heart.

Nelly

Marnie is beastly. Not a word of thanks for the beautiful dinner I made and then giving out to Lennie, who was only speaking the truth. How could she imagine for a minute they had loved us? They didn't love us. They've ruined us, and damn them for it. Unfortunate creatures, their ghastly bodies rotting on our lawn, fouling up the neighborhood. I can't imagine why R. T. Macdonald should want to find them at all. He is beginning a new life and yet he seeks to pair it to a couple of bothersome fools. Bothersome I say.

Lennie

Journey back home was long and moody. Marnie barely said two words until Glasgow and then made some small talk about the city being beautiful or something like it. I knew the sulk was over when we threw each other a couple of apologetic smiles. I was so relieved and then less so when we arrived to a business card from Robert T. Macdonald urging us to call him upon our return and in block capitals if you can imagine such a thing. We don't need him, really we don't. He knows the girls are in my care until someone other than him says they're not. They're certainly in no hurry to shack up with Grandpa and wait for their elusive parents' return. The man doesn't have a clue.

It was Marnie who called him but he didn't want to talk on the phone and asked to come round. We were all reluctant at first. Marnie has exams to study for, even though I never see her do too much of it and if I'm being honest it's a worry. No one's that bright.

It was an hour after the call when he arrived and in quite a rage.

"Where the hell have you been?" he demanded.

"What's it to you?" says Marnie.

"What's it to me? I'm your grandfather for blazes' sake. You can't just go off and not tell a person where you've been."

We all looked to the other and mutually agreed not to tell him.

"We were in Mull," said Marnie.

"Mull?" he repeated. "What's in Mull?" he snips.

"Peace and quiet, old boy," says Nelly in her way.

Nelly's manner clearly irritated him but not as much as her evident sarcasm.

"I was worried sick. I almost called the police."

This seemed to shake the girls.

"And then what?" said Marnie.

He looked blank. Hadn't thought of that, had he.

"And then I'd find you, wouldn't I?"

The idea he had a right to *find* them irked both girls, but Marnie remained calm.

"Do you understand we're in Lennie's care until Izzy and Gene return?" Marnie tells him.

He nodded, but it was obvious he understood no such thing.

"And they're okay with you just going off without a word to anyone?"

"As a matter of fact they are. This was something we'd planned a long time before you arrived on the scene."

"I'm sorry," he said. "I was just worried, that's all, one minute you're here and the next you're not."

"I don't mean to be rude," Nelly pipes up. "But you do realize we just met you and not so long ago."

"I know that but I'm your grandfather, I have a right to see my own blood and know where they are."

"Actually you don't," I interrupt. "The girls are in my care and your daughter hadn't really approved the visitation you believe you are entitled to. Now if you don't mind Marnie has her studies and I have dinner to make."

"You've told her I'm here?" he asked, assuming we'd talked to her, and of course the answer is no, but we don't tell him that and so Marnie and Nelly gave one another "the look" again.

"She doesn't like to be bothered when she's working. Doesn't even have a mobile," says Marnie. "Anyway she'd have a fit if she knew you were here, probably come back and stop us even talking to you."

He reddened and not with embarrassment but with rage.

"Perhaps we can have another brunch sometime," suggested Nelly.

"I'd like that, maybe with both of you?"

He looked hopefully to Marnie and she just shrugged, she doesn't care squat for the fellow. We all made yawning sounds after that and fortunately he knew where he wasn't wanted and left with his pretend brunch suggestion tucked safely under his hat, at least I hope it was pretend.

Marnie

Our trip to Firemore certainly ruffled the feathers of Robert T. Macdonald but we handled it. What does he expect, this guy? We don't know anything about him, and what we do know about him isn't that nice. He beat his family and drank like a fish. I know he says he's changed but what do we really know about him? Of course Nelly's all over him after a very successful breakfast date. She's so crazy, that girl. I tried to explain to her why we can't get too close to him and had to actually remind her Izzy and Gene are dead, they haven't gone on holiday at all and that they're under the flower beds. We had to move Izzy again but to the side of the house, we dug her a little grave and put rocks on her, but then we moved the rocks because it looked like an actual grave, which meant getting more and more plants, but to be honest that also looked weird because there's no light at the side of the house and plants need light, don't they? We left it though, it was better than the shed. Lennie's dog just wouldn't leave it alone.

Anyway I went and saw Vlado. I need my job back. I can't pay the rent. I can't buy anything. People will come. The Social and R. T. Macdonald if we're not careful. We'll be evicted and then everyone will find out where Gene and Izzy are. That Vlado's really fucked things up for me.

Turns out he lives off Byres Road. He doesn't have a buzzer

so I know straightaway it's a shit hole. There's some stinking old guy sleeping under a pile of greasy newspapers, well he looked old, he could have been ten for all I knew. Dirt hides a multitude of sins. I heard Bono giving it plenty from the flat at the top, figured I'd start there. Sure enough it was him, Mr. V. Pavlovic as scrawled on a Post-it and then taped to the door.

I knocked on Vlado's door for like five minutes. The music was blaring. Eventually he answers but he's obviously not too happy to see me.

"What do you want here?" he says.

"You got Mick to sack me," I say.

"You're too young to sell drugs, to have anything to do with drugs. Go home to your books," he says.

"I need the money."

"Then get a job," he yells.

"I had a job," I scream.

"Not anymore, little girl. Go home!"

"I'm not a little girl. I'm almost sixteen. You go home."

Then I burst into tears, which made him uncomfortable. I could see he wanted to close the door in my face, but he also wanted me to stop crying.

"What kind of things can you do?" he asks.

"I don't know," I say.

"Everyone can do something. You have to be resourceful in this life."

"Like you?"

"I am in a very different situation from you. My choices are limited in this country. I do what I have to do."

"My choices are limited."

"Your parents they have jobs?"

"No."

"They have problems?"

"They're never around. I need to earn money. Pay the rent."

"The government pays the rent, no?"

He had an answer for everything.

"To them, not me. They spend all the money. I have to take care of my sister. Keep us from being homeless. I needed that job."

Now he feels bad.

"I see what I can do," he says.

"You'll speak to Mick?"

"I don't want you anywhere near Mick, understand?"

I nod.

"You come back tomorrow. Seven o'clock. In the morning."

"Why?"

"You want to work?"

I nod.

"Then be here in the morning." He slams the door.

Next day I show at seven, as instructed. I make myself nice. Summer makeup, best shoes, and a cute bag.

He answers the door like I'm late. I'm not. Then he looks me up and down and starts to laugh.

"I have something to match your shoes," he says. That makes me excited until he hands me a red bucket.

"Come in," he says. "But take the silly shoes off."

He says his floors are wooden and he doesn't want me denting them.

His house is like an IKEA showroom. Everything's either beech wood or black. Don't get me wrong, he has it nice, I just didn't expect it. The stairs to his house are a little deceptive because his flat is lovely. He has a beautiful big bay window facing onto the street and a really nice fireplace with lots of pictures on the mantel. I want to take a closer look at the photos, but I know he wouldn't like that and so I keep my distance.

"You will clean my house," he says. "Every week and not looking like little hooker. I have neighbors."

"Clean your own fucking house," I say and throw the bucket at him. He thinks this is hilarious and hands me back the bucket.

"Take it. Five hours a week every Saturday morning. A hundred pounds."

"Five hours. That's it!" I say.

"You are on substitute time," he says, but he was waving his hand around like he wasn't too sure what he was saying, English being his second language and all that.

"What do you mean, substitute time?" I know he's got something wrong and I want to rub his face in it, make him embarrassed.

"You know, I am testing you."

"You mean probationary period."

"If it means I will fire you if you can't clean my house then this is the right word."

Then he gave me a list and left. It was a pretty big list if you want to know. I had to do his laundry, change his sheets, wipe down his DVDs and CDs 'cause the guy doesn't know what a cover is for, they were all over the place, it took ages. Then I checked out his pictures. It was him and a girl my age. They looked like each other and so I knew it was his daughter. Cleaning up I saw lots of other pictures of him and his wife and his daughter or who I supposed to be his daughter.

There were also toddler snaps. You can tell tons from pictures. I found out he grew up on a farm with his parents and had an older brother or maybe it was a cousin. On his wall in his bedroom he had a certificate from a university in chemistry and he had lots of soccer trophies and lots of books. He's a bit of a reader. Also he doesn't wear aftershave, he wears sandalwood oil and he wears contacts, so I deduced his appearance must be important to him and so is sex because I found a jumbo box of Durex behind the toilet. That's pretty much all the information I could glean from cleaning his house. All his bills are paid 'cause he has this little board where he sticks the receipts and where my £100 will always be in a little yellow envelope with MISS MARNIE written on the front.

Nelly

While Marnie goes to Lochgilphead with her wayward girlfriends I take the opportunity to get to know our grandfather Robert T. Macdonald at his workshop situated in the Barrowland, a marketplace selling fish and bread and all kinds of bric-a-brac.

He shows us around his studio softened by woodchip and hardened by oak. He is working on a headboard. The headboard is for me. It is beautifully carved with stars. I can't help but adore it.

"What do you think, love?" he asks with a familiarity not quite earned yet but I don't seem to mind.

"Many thanks, Robert," I say, although my gratitude does seem to startle him.

He has a young apprentice with him. Robert greets him warmly.

"This is Sandy," he says. "My apprentice."

He was a very pleasant lad and strangely familiar to me, not that I got a chance to quiz the fellow for he ran off and with the greatest of haste to fetch some milk, which was a rather pointless feat given we hadn't even been offered a cup of tea. Thank goodness for Lennie's cake in the oven for I was suddenly very tired of the workshop and very keen to return home, but not wishing to offend anyone we invite Robert T. Macdonald to sup with us. He was overwhelmed with gratitude and so I knew immediately we had done the right thing.

Lennie

It was a few minutes before he recognized me. I was quicker. It was his eyes that gave him away, violet. I remember them from the back of the police car, the mascara trickling over his cheeks and his red hair, scooped into a ponytail. It was cut short now and washed. He was a handsome lad but he was a boy. I could see it then. He was wearing a black cotton T-shirt with words I couldn't read. I can't read much these days. Suddenly his eyes pass across my shoes, I always wear these shoes, they're white rimmed with red laces, they're your shoes, and we were always the same size. His eyes scan the rest of me until they reach my own eyes. He staggers a little, thinks of staying, faking, pretending and when he can't he runs under the pretense of a forgotten errand. I am frozen to the spot and no one has noticed. In haste I announce, "I have a cake in the oven." Robert T. Macdonald is quietly furious and knowing I must appease him I invite him to dinner. It does the trick nicely and within fifteen minutes we are in the car and on our way home. On arrival it is noted there is no cake; I go to the bathroom and I am sick to my stomach. When I return to the kitchen Nelly and Robert T. Macdonald are thrown together at the sink, peeling potatoes; there is laughter and closeness. It makes me nervous for her, it makes me scared for us all.

Marnie

In Lochgilphead all the houses are painted white and it's full of old people, like a lot of old people, they're everywhere, mowing around like Daleks, carrying their shopping in giant canvas bags. Old people never use plastic bags. I don't know why that is.

It's a small town and has a clean freshness about it and pure. My senses welcomed it. The house is reeking right now even though I've washed it like a thousand times. Nelly says she can't smell anything, that it's all in my head, but I don't care what she says, it's my hands chapped from the bleach.

It's good to leave Glasgow every now and then, sometimes I go to an island called Rothesay, I take a train to Wemyss Bay and the ferry over to Bute. To be honest I've only been a few times. Once with Nana Lou, once with Gene and Izzy, but they got pissed on the boat over and went straight to a bar, leaving Nelly and me on the Esplanade with money for chips, and once with Susie and Kim. We had a right laugh and got totally pished. We went for a walk in this wood overlooking the sea. It was nice and had an amazing view. We watched the boat leaving the harbor and then coming back again. Then we carved our names into a couple of trees, scratched would be more accurate. We met a couple of guys arsing around on a swing, they were the same age as us, but they didn't hang about long. One of them was really nice-looking and Susie was all over him, but you could see he wasn't into it. He wouldn't even snog her and said he had to go home for his tea. Then she got nasty and called him a fag, that's when his mate threw a clump of dirt at her, Kim went mad at that and was right after him, she pinned him to the ground and smacked him in the gob. The Looker comes to his mate's rescue, almost in tears and said they wanted to go home. I felt bad for them then, even though guys shouldn't act like that, all weepy and scared, a couple of pussies they were. Anyway we let them go. Told them not to come back to the wood or we'd kill them. Then they ran away like deer do when they hear a twig snap in a wood. When they were gone we found their soccer cards, they must have been trading them, imagine that, fourteen-year-old guys collecting cards. Wouldn't last five minutes in the Urban Kingdom.

Kim totally hated Lochgilphead, she's a Glaswegian through and through, she said it was like a Scottish Stepford and couldn't wait to get away from the place. Lorna loved it and bought a ton of rock, I love that stuff. Makes your tongue pink and your breath minty, but we weren't there for the rock we were there for Susie. She wanted to see her mum; she was in the local psychiatric unit.

Susie was nervous as fuck on the bus. She'd asked her granny if she could go, but her granny said no and forbade Susie to ever mention it again, but none of us thought that was fair. She can't keep Susie away from her own flesh and blood and she hasn't seen her mother since she was three years old. She keeps a picture of her though, in her purse.

Susie didn't want us to go to the hospital with her, she wanted to do it alone, and so we waited for her in town.

We tried to get into a pub and have something to eat, but the barman wouldn't serve us. Kim went mental. We only wanted a sandwich, maybe a beer if he was up for it, but he wasn't. Kim called him a prick. A bloke at the bar chipped in, "Away and get yourself an ice cream." Kim went nuts. "Come here and say that, ya wanker" and actually wanted to fight a grown man, take him outside and give him a kicking. The barman burst his hole. "No need for that, Zorro. Away you go." The bloke in the bar was killing himself, thought Kim was the funniest person he'd ever met in his life and let's face it she'd made a bit of a tit of herself. We had to drag her away in the end.

Eventually we found an off license, a grubby wee place, selling everything from kids' toys to sliced ham. Lorna had a fake ID on her, also she paid with a debit card, so he was willing to suspend disbelief and sell us a bottle of vodka. We also got six cans of Coke and took it to the nearest toilet, poured half the juice out the can and filled the rest with booze.

It should have been a good laugh, but it wasn't. Kim's been off her meds for about a fortnight now and she's been a nightmare. A total head case. Slightest thing can cause offense. Her and Lorna have been fighting like cat and dog. Lorna says she can't handle it. She's also going on about being bisexual, she's driving Kim mad. At one point I thought we were going to get chucked off the bus, especially when Kim shouts, "If you eat pussy you're a lezzy in my book."

Lorna was mortified. "It's more complicated than that."

Kim goes, "Is it fuck."

"Sexuality, politics, and religion, these are not things a polite person debates with another."

"Religion," says Kim. "Don't make me laugh. Bible is a lot of bull."

I suppose it should be awkward two folk fighting about pussy and the word of God, but I'm used to it, people tearing lumps out of each other. Susie told them both to shut up. She probably didn't want the rest of the bus thinking she was a lezzy too. I know I didn't.

We thought we'd have to wait ages for Susie but she was back in about an hour looking kind of blank with absolutely nothing in her face to show how it went. Eventually we asked how her mum was, but she said she didn't want to talk about it. Lorna suggested we go get something to eat. We were starving and the bus back to Glasgow was still a couple of hours away, but Kim said it was inappropriate to eat. Lorna told her to piss off and stomped off to the nearest tearoom. I stayed with Kim, but I really wanted to go with Lorna. Susie just sat there, not saying a word, but after about ten minutes she starts to breathe funny and then she starts to cry. Kim gave Susie a big hug and held her for a long time. Something horrible had happened, that much we had worked out. At first I thought her mum was dead, but she wasn't. Turns out she's not even in the psychiatric unit. They didn't know who Ivy Murphy was and when Susie got home to her granny, her granny had to tell her the truth. Her mum lives in Croydon and has a new family. She has two boys, one called Noah and the other one Peter. She also has a husband called Mike. Her granny had wedding pictures and pictures of her mum with her kids and on holidays with her kids and on beaches with her kids. And there were letters, a ton of letters, but her granny didn't want Susie to read them. Susie went mental over that and so her granny gave in. I suppose they were nice letters really, the kind of letters a mother should get from a daughter. Her mum was obviously doing well in life. Talked about her kids and the house her husband had built, talked about the places they'd been and the places they were going to. Her worries about the future, about getting her kids into good schools and bird flu. She was really worried about bird flu. And there were loads of thank-you notes for gifts her granny had sent to her grandchildren. There wasn't a single word about Susie in any of the letters. Nothing, like she didn't even exist, and if that wasn't bad enough, there was one letter written last year about how brilliant it had been to see Susie's granny after such a long time, how the boys missed her, and how she hoped Susie's granny would visit them again. Susie went demented. Her granny told her she'd gone to Butlins. Susie started tearing the house apart, and her granny just sat there, letting her kick the shit out of walls, doors, and windows. It was a neighbor who called the police. Her granny was in a right state. Susie had to be pinned to the floor by Kim.

When I go see her the next day at her granny's Susie doesn't say anything for ages. Then she goes, "Where the fuck's Gene?"

"Don't know," I say, but the whole time I'm wondering, Why does she want to know about Gene at a time like this?

"We're getting married," she says.

"Excuse me?" I say.

"I said we're getting married, me and Gene, soon as I'm sixteen. We're in love, so I know he's not in Turkey with your fucking ma."

"What are you talking about?"

She produces two plane tickets to Spain, one with her name on it, the other with Gene's.

I can't move.

"We were going to disappear, start a new life away from this shit hole. That's why I went to see my ma, to say goodbye." She was sad then, but I didn't care. I wanted to wring her neck. I wanted to do a lot of things but in that moment I could barely move a muscle.

"When the fuck did this happen?" I yelled.

"Started last summer. I went to see you and you weren't in. He was. We have a lot in common as a matter of fact."

"Shut up," I says.

"He's not with her, Marnie, I know he's not, something's happened to him."

"Nothing's happened to him, he's done a runner like he always does."

"Then why's his stuff still in the house? Last time he texted me he said he loved me. We were meant to meet up the next day. Go to Spain. That was months ago. He bought the fucking tickets!" she screamed.

She started flapping them about in my face.

I didn't know what to say but I had to find something, anything to keep her from raising the alarm and going to the police.

"He'll be back," I assured her. "But not for you," I spat.

"I'm going to the police," she says.

"You do that Gene gets done for rape of a minor. Abduction probably. You're only fifteen."

"They don't have to know that."

"You think I won't tell them? You can't be breaking up my family and expect me to do nothing." Obviously I was a little wobbly on this point.

Susie cried like a baby after that and I wanted to hug her, but I couldn't. She made me sick to my stomach.

After the Susie bombshell I went to the library. Drowned my sorrows in algebra, I have prelims right now and I can barely think with everything going on. Anyway when I got home Kirkland was hanging around my gate, earphones on, black coat hanging around his legs and big smiles. I couldn't be arsed with him.

"What you doing here, don't you have to study or something or is that just me?" I says.

"Come to give you this," he says and hands me a CD.

I say, "Thanks," but really I'm thinking, *Another fucking compilation. Great.*

"Did you get my text messages?" he asks.

"Yeah."

"So do you want to go and see a film?"

"If I'd wanted to see a film, I'd have texted you back, but I didn't text you back."

"How no?" he says, obviously not taking the hint.

"'Cause I don't want to see a film, Fannybaws."

"Did I do something wrong?" he whimpers.

Now I feel like I'm pointing a shotgun at a puppy.

"Look," I say. "You're a nice bloke and I feel like a bitch saying this, but I'm not into you, okay?"

He doesn't say anything for a bit, then he goes, "Got any jellies?"

"You need to see Mick for that stuff. I don't work for him anymore."

"Can we at least be friends?"

"Aye awright."

What else am I going to say?

Then he steps in for a hug and throwing him a bone, I hug him back, but then he moves in for a snog.

"Fuck off," I says.

"I'm sorry," he says, but he's not. Chancer.

"So you should be," I say and then I stomp off. Very dramatic, but when I keek out the window I see him holding his head like he's in this big love drama and I've totally fucked him up or something. All this after one awkward shag, but that's how shags are the first time, everyone trying to impress and getting it wrong.

I knew I had to get rid of him then. I mean really rid of him. I don't want him thinking about me and decide to be brutal. When it comes to guys like Kirkland you've got to be. It's for their own good. So the following Saturday we're all out at this club, Kirkland in his finest goth attire, black suit jacket instead of the signature trampy mac he likes to wear. He even washed his hair, he actually looked smart and was wearing aftershave and nice stuff, he usually stinks of patchouli incense, an arse of a smell. Anyway I have a job to do and so I single out his mate Daniel and take him out back for a BJ, but I can't face it 'cause he reeks and I snog him instead. Kirkland thinks he's best friends with Daniel but that's the thing with Kirkland, you give him any attention whatsoever and suddenly he's your bitch. Anyway when we get back to the club I find Kirkland getting off with some random Indie chick with pink hair and it bugs me. In a very surprising fury I go and get myself a drink, mostly to get the taste of Danny out my mouth and Kirkland appears at my side.

"Awright," he says. "Good night?"

"Great," I says. "Your pal has a big dick."

"Right?" he says.

"Who the fuck's she?" I say and like I'm annoyed. I want to kick myself for that, but it's too late, it's out of my mouth and he thinks he's got me all interested, but I'm not.

"What do you care?" he says.

"I don't." Trying to take back any notion I give a shit. " 'Cause I don't."

"Good. Want a drink?"

"Okay," and he buys me a drink. He's like that. Then he takes it over to the table for me and sits next to her.

His pal Danny's all over me of course and can't snog for shit and Pink's all over Kirkland, then I remember what a nice kisser Kirkland is and I can't stop looking at him. Then I notice he's looking at me while he's kissing Pink. It gets really sick then and we're kissing these people we obviously don't want to be kissing, our hands reaching past them on the sofa, playing with each other's fingers. I can't take it anymore and go to the toilet and see if Kirkland will follow me and he does. We just stand there, staring and suddenly I'm feeling this warm sensation from my loins to my lips and I jump him, I want to feel him everywhere and it's so red we have to leave the club or rather run away from Pink and Danny, who end up getting off with each other and bitching about us probably.

Anyway we got to Kirkland's house and we take a ton of Mick's drugs or Kirkland does and we fuck all night and it might be the first time in my life I actually want to do it with someone and it's different, naked, real, careful, and honest.

I can hardly believe it. I thought I hated him, but it was a lie and I told it to myself, why would I do that?

His parents were away and so I stay with him for two amazing days of eating and shagging, all the time some CD he's recorded for me, maybe five, spinning in the background. He tells me he loves me and has always loved me, he tells me he will always love me and I don't say it back and just laugh at him, but he doesn't care, he still says it and I want him to. When it's time to go, I want to stay, but I pretend I want to go and when I look for my clothes, they're all folded, even my pants, makes me a wee bit embarrassed, so I act cool and call him a soppy arse, but Kirkland doesn't know what cool means, he's so straight and then he does this really cute begging thing and taking the piss out of himself for wanting me to stay and that makes me want to stay more. But I can't, I don't want to make him like me too much or maybe I don't want to like him too much.

I don't have my iPod on me and so he gives me his.

Outside it's freezing, but it's a good cold. He walks me to the subway and we pass this window, it's all shiny and like a mirror, reflecting me and Kirkland holding hands. He's taller than me and we look quite funny together, then he says, "Don't you like how we look?" I don't say anything, but then he goes, "'Cause I like how we look." Then he pulls me to his face and we kiss again.

On the way home I listen to everything he played for me over the weekend and even though it doesn't sound the way it did when we were together, it sounds like something I want to hear all the time.

Next day I go to see Susie but I can't ring the doorbell. I don't even know why I'm at the door at all to be honest. I suppose I want to tell my bezzy mate all about Kirkland, someone who won't say anything and be glad for me, someone who'll keep it a secret, but things are too fucked-up between Susie and me and so I leave. I decide to find Kim, but she's all gutted over Lorna, they've had another barney and so I end up comforting Kim and saying shite like "She's just not worth it" when I should be saying, "Take your fucking meds, you mental head," but she's my bezzy so I don't say anything, I just hug her and hand her hankies. In the end I go to the garden and tell Izzy, she could never keep a secret before, but given her situation she's great at keeping secrets. So is Gene, but then again he always was.

Nelly

Marnie has taken up with a boy. I've seen them from my window. He takes her home almost every night, a true gentleman. Sometimes they lurk in the shadows where I can't see them. I wonder at their secrets. He must be a very humorous chap, for she giggles and gasps at everything he has to say. She is positively smitten with the fellow. I have no interest in boys. They smell of socks and oil. Their teeth are yellow and their smiles too wide. I wish they'd look to their books, I wish they wouldn't whistle and gawk, I wish they wouldn't look at me at all. It is most vexing.

"Enjoy it while it lasts, hot stuff," says Sharon.

"Don't call me that," I tell her.

"Hot?" She laughs. "What's your problem? You're gorgeous. Could have any guy you want and you act like a freak."

"You have a fellow no doubt," I say.

"I have several fellows, my lady."

"I have more important pursuits in life."

"What can be more important than having a good time? You're not forty. You should hang with us sometime. It would be a laugh."

I shrug.

"Suit yourself, freakoid."

I was ever so relieved as she walked away, I returned to calm and rushed home to Lennie. We can play together and eat crumble. It's exactly what the doctor ordered. A crumble and a violin. It doesn't get much better than that.

Lennie

Couldn't believe the verdict. Brain tumor. Malignant. Aggressive. Too large for surgery they said. I didn't know what to say. I felt a strange tingling in my fingertips and my tongue went sour. My body felt heavy and my head light. I tried to stand up and go home, take what he said and fold it into a drawer, but I couldn't even stand and had to sit, someone handed me water while another talked to me of hospices on account of having no one to care for me and it's true there isn't anyone. I can't exactly lean on the girls, can I? They mustn't even know.

I feel a terrible grief when I think of passing on, and fear, so much fear, but it's best not to think of such things I suppose. I could still live a long time, doctor says it happens, although he didn't look too optimistic when I asked him, he still smiled at me, albeit a paltry smile, but still, it lends a little comfort.

I have much to organize now. Affairs to get in order and a life to tidy away. Doesn't seem real all of this. Doesn't feel real at all, but then something taps at me and shows me the truth, I'll fall over or break a cup and then it all comes swimming back to me, the doctors, the tumor, and the weak smiles.

I hope to die in my sleep, Joseph, not knowing, just closing my eyes and forgetting the things I am leaving behind. I don't want to die with my heart breaking. I don't want to die at all.

Marnie

It was a gorgeous morning and I was in the garden. I don't smell them so much anymore or maybe I'm used to it or my senses are pretending it's something else, maybe I am.

Nelly was over at Lennie's so I could mellow with a CD Kirkland made, have a fag, and text my boyfriend.

That's when I heard it. Noise, coming from inside the house, barging into my Sunday. I thought I was imagining it at first but then I heard a voice, an angry voice. I wanted to go over to Lennie's, skip over the fence, but he'd have called the police and that's the last thing I needed, not with two dead bodies in the garden. I wondered if it was a burglar or a junkie looking for something random to steal, a lot of it about round here. Then I got scared it was a rapist and I'm searching frantically for an exit but there wasn't one, I couldn't go to Lennie's and I couldn't scale the walls surrounding our house. I was stuck with nowhere to go and I really didn't want to get raped, so I hid in the shed.

It was freezing in the shed and of course it made me think of Izzy hanging from the rafters and I felt kind of ill, sort of sick in my stomach. I felt her then and for the first time in a long time, as if she was standing right next to me, but she wasn't. I heard footsteps, there was someone in the garden and they were making strides toward the shed, I was like a rat in a cage and my heart was ready to explode and my teeth ready to bite. I grabbed a hammer and got ready to defend, I closed my eyes, I was afraid of what I'd see and then the door opened and it was Mick, not a rapist or a burglar, just Mick looking confused and a bit scared of the hammer.

"What you doing in here?" he says in a curious inquiry kind of way.

"Fuck, Mick. I thought you were a rapist or something. You scared the shit out of me." I push him hard in the chest. "How did you get in anyway?" I says.

"You left the front door open. What's that fucking smell by the way?" he says, sniffing at the air.

"Sewers." I tremble. "They're fucked."

"Naw, that's not it. S'like a hospital smell. Disinfectant over shite."

I shove past him, into the house.

"Where you going?" he asks.

"I'm not going anywhere, you are. I want you out of my house."

"Is that right?" He laughs.

He follows me into the living room.

"What you doing here anyway?" I says.

"Looking for Gene. What do you think?"

"I told you, he's with Izzy. They're in Turkey."

"Then what's this?"

He waves Gene's passport in the air. Izzy's passport.

"Where did you get that?" I try not to shake. I try not to vomit.

"Shoe box in the airing cupboard."

I'm shivering now and not from cold.

"Look," he says, "I'm not going to hurt you, okay? I just want to know where they are and you're going to tell me, Marnie, 'cause I'm not leaving this house till you do."

I had a feeling he'd say that.

Lennie

She came out of the shed with a hammer in her hand. I rather hoped she'd smack him with it. No such intelligence. They had a wee chat and then they went inside, but she didn't look that happy about it. Poor lassie, doesn't know her arse from her elbow and you want to help her but you know she'll lock the doors if you try and I need them open to comfort her when she's had enough, when she's too tired to pretend anymore. She's obviously looking for a father figure, and love perhaps; she just looks in the wrong place and almost on purpose. That's probably why she turned to him in the first place, seeking pain and feeding the loathing within. It makes me frightened for her, it's like there's wood rot inside her eating away at her soul and nibbling at all the things she could become; fortunately for her I'm a bit of a handyman in this respect and this particular wood rot is very treatable. In the right hands of course.

There's a number on his van. I remember. MAKE YOUR DAY SPECIAL. CALL MICK.

Time to call his wife I think. Make her day special.

Nelly

In the middle of what was a beautiful duet Lennie is distracted by something outside. It is the first time in a long time Lennie has been able to play from beginning to end and in tempo, I am utterly thrilled and then heartily disappointed when I find he has stopped to look out the window into our nasty old garden. When I look over his shoulder, however, I see what he must see. Bobby. A limb in his mouth. Without the slightest hesitation Lennie immediately finds the telephone and I am quite panicked. I wonder in vain why Marnie and her friend can't see what I am seeing. We will be captured I am sure of it. I must pack our bags immediately for we must run.

Marnie

He ripped the house apart, feathers everywhere. Tore the back of the sofa with a pocket knife and turned every cupboard and every mattress in the house upside down, except Izzy and Gene's, which we had disposed of already.

"Whir's their fucking mattress?" he yelled.

"Gene got rid of it," I say.

"Why?"

"It had shit on it. All the way through."

"Filthy bastard," he says and then continues on his rampage.

Eventually he came across the bleach in the cupboard under the stairs. We have liters of the stuff.

"You expecting the plague or something?" he says.

Then he goes to the side of the house where we buried Izzy. I got really scared then and I was sure he was going to find her but then I receive a blow to the head and I'm on the floor with someone behind me, yelling, "Fuck monster!" I covered my skull with both hands, like I'm expecting a bomb to explode and for about a minute I don't know what the fuck's going on, someone's kicking at me, calling me a slag and telling Mick he's a bastard. And he is.

"Julie, stop! For fuck's sake!" Mick screams. He was doing everything he could to get her off me but she was raging and her anger made her strong.

"I'm going to kill her. I'm going to fucking kill her."

More kicking.

"For gawd's sake. Let her go."

The kicking stops and she turns her attention to Mick. Starts slapping him, screaming, throwing anything she can get her hands on, crap things mostly, but heavy, a snow globe with the Loch Ness Monster inside, a dictionary and a couple of candlesticks, a toaster and a pot, some pans and cutlery, the place is a tip and I'm curled up in the corner terrified and crying. That's when Robert T. Macdonald turns up.

"What's going on?" he yells.

Mick is hiding behind the sofa, Julie's ready to pap a frying pan at him.

"Who the fuck are you?" snaps Julie.

"I'm Marnie's grandfather. Who are you?"

"Well your granddaughter's a whore. *A. Whore.*"

Robert T. Macdonald scans the room and sees Mick skulking in the background, he looks right at me and stunned he goes, "This guy?"

I nod.

"For gawd's sake, lassie," he says in this disapproving tone and that pisses me off, it's not like he's earned it yet. I want to tell him to fuck off, I want to tell him it's got nothing to do with him, but I need him to stop everything, I need him to help me 'cause there isn't anyone else.

I nod and hear myself say, "Sorry."

"It's not what you think," says Mick.

"And what do I think, Mister?" says Robert T. Macdonald.

"I'm just looking for Gene."

"He's in Turkey with Isabel."

"And how did they get there? With a raft?" says Mick and produces the passports. Robert T. Macdonald grabs them, opens them, and examines them, and then he stares at me, looking guilty as fuck.

"I don't know where they are," I whisper.

"She's still a whore!" yells Julie.

"Leave," commands Robert T. Macdonald.

"He's got my money. Gene, he's got it," says Mick.

"Then you shouldn't have given it to him, should you?"

"I'm not leaving here till I know where he is," says Mick.

"Lassie says she doesn't know."

"Well somebody knows."

"Out of here," says Robert T. Macdonald.

Mick feels brave now. "And who's going to make me?"

That's when Robert T. Macdonald leaps across the table and takes him by the throat, squeezes his neck like it's a tube of toothpaste. Mick's mouth widens and his eyes water and it looks like Robert T. Macdonald's going to kill him, but then Julie smacks him with the frying pan, knocking him unconscious to the floor. Thinking they've killed him, Julie and Mick take off in Mick's ice cream van. Next thing Lennie arrives on the scene and thinks we need to get Robert T. Macdonald to a doctor, but Robert T. Macdonald comes to and says he'll go himself. Lennie makes him tea and tries to tidy up, but there's no point, everything's broken or torn and there's no mending to be done, just damage, everywhere you look.

"Where are they?" demands Robert T. Macdonald.

"They took off in Mick's van," I say.

"Not those fools, where is Izzy? Where is Gene?"

And I want to tell him everything. I want to tell Lennie

everything. I want to tell him Gene and Izzy are buried in the garden. I want to tell him I've been selling ice creams and drugs and shagging a married man. I want to tell him how tired I am and how I wish I was the one buried in the garden and let it all go, but as soon as I open my mouth Nelly turns up and goes, "Whose child is this?"

Mick and Julie forgot their baby.

Half an hour later Julie hurls herself through the front door and grabs her child gurgling in his car seat and then flips us all the finger.

"How unladylike," says Nelly.

"Fuck you," says Julie. "Fuck all of you."

Lennie

As always, Marnie was fast to explain their absence, although not fast enough for Robert T. Macdonald.

"They've just gone," said Marnie. "I don't know where."

"But you knew about the money," said Robert T. Macdonald.

"Mick told me."

"S'drug money, isn't it?" he said.

She nods.

"You get about, don't you?" spat Robert T. Macdonald.

"What fucking business is it of yours?" screamed Marnie.

"Like it or not, young lady, I am your grandfather and this lying won't stand, the company you keep won't stand, and living here in this guy's house won't stand either. Where are they?"

"I don't know."

"I could go to the authorities," he said.

"You'll get Izzy done if you do that. Is that what you want? She could go to jail."

"How could she just leave you like that?" There was hurt in his voice, disappointment.

"You can talk," spat Marnie.

"I left her with her mother. S'not the same."

"Her mother died. She was completely alone in the world. No wonder she dived into Gene's arms. S'all your fault this."

Marnie was close to tears. The day's events had been too much for her I could tell and I can't pretend I didn't enjoy the attack on Robert T. Macdonald.

"Come come, Marnie, too late to be throwing stones now," says Nelly from the quietest corner of the room and holding a suitcase.

"They'll be back. They always come back. Chin up, old girl," she assures her.

Marnie looked incredulous and as stunned as I was by Nelly's impromptu bravado.

"I say we all sit down, have a nice piece of cake, a cup of tea perhaps. Would you oblige us, Lennie?"

"Of course," I said. "It would be my pleasure," but it was no such thing.

Nelly

I didn't know what to do with myself or my suitcase.

There was Bobby, bringing what looked like a knee into Lennie's front room and my sister selling confectionery to the dismay of an unbalanced spouse.

I was a nervous wreck, surely I was. Retrieving the bone and burying it again was no easy feat. I didn't even know which grave he'd pulled it from.

Thank goodness for Lennie's tea and cake. It certainly took the edge off what had been a horrific day for us all. Marnie eventually simmered down and Robert T. Macdonald requested we spend more time with him until Izzy returns. Since Marnie knows this will mean a lifetime she was somewhat reluctant to agree, but I was more enthused in this respect. He had saved the day after all. It couldn't hurt anyone to spend a leisurely afternoon taking a walk for example and our breakfast together had been a great success and so we made arrangements. Marnie made her excuses of course and I was very disappointed. He'd stood up for and protected her, heaven help us all if he hadn't.

Marnie is not the strength she has been in my life; in fact she is failing me in too many ways. I hardly see her around these days. I can't imagine what occupies her, not when there is work to be done, secrets to be kept, and people to account for. Grandfather is evidently a liability, and if his daughter doesn't show up soon then we'll all be in hot water. Piping hot!

Marnie

Handle with care is the line I'm taking with Robert T. Macdonald. One false move and we're done. Nelly was wide eyed and question free for a change. She didn't want to know about Julie and Mick, for example, or any of the things I know she heard like the drugs or the affair with a married man, although she did want to know how long I had been selling ice cream.

"I'm not selling it anymore," I told her.

"Excellent news," she says. "It's fattening, isn't it, and terribly bad for the complexion."

"But Gene liked it, didn't he?" I say.

"I couldn't exactly say," she whispers.

I could have screamed.

Now she wants to make cozy with Robert T. Macdonald just because he played Batman for the day and when she doesn't know the first thing about him. None of us do.

Nelly

Lennie is entirely bothersome. Always taking off somewhere. Very secretive. Perhaps he has a girlfriend? Fortunately we have our gramps to keep an eye on us. He's always around and with a helping hand. How badly I feel for the lies we must tell him to keep our own secrets.

We've had a jolly nice time of late and have been so many wonderful places together. He knows Glasgow like the back of his hand. He likes to go to St. Mary's. It holds an especially important place in his heart with its vaulted ceilings and hand-crafted oak pews. I am permitted to play on the altar by Father McKeown, a true Irishman and a real character. He says the music is positively celestial. This fills Gramps with such pride. How he glows. Father McKeown says I have a great deal to offer the church, as does Gramps, who had apparently considered the priesthood in his youth. Such a shame for I believe he would have made an excellent priest. Excellent.

Lennie

The ice cream vendor's wife called round yesterday afternoon while I looked for my shoes. Your shoes. I can't find them anywhere and I can't go outside without them, it's wet and it's cold. I'll freeze. She was a little haughty to tell the truth and I wasn't best pleased to see her, though it took me a while to place her, most vexing. I thought she'd come for another go at Marnie but that wasn't the case at all. Her husband has gone missing and it seems he has wiped out what remained of the money they kept in their bank account. A real gent. She made sure not to call while the girls were at home and was secretly hoping I'd seen him around. He's obviously running from someone and I hope they catch him; he doesn't deserve to breathe, a man like that. All she has left is their little baby and the van of course. I told her to run it herself, branch out a little. She seemed quite taken by the idea, not that it's my business. I couldn't care less where the blaggard's hiding. I've got my own problems.

Marnie

Mick's disappeared and everyone is looking for him including Vlado, but he's gone. Vlado has passed the matter on to his associates and the search is wide. If he so much as sets foot on Glasgow terrain it better be with a bagful of cash or he'll get the shit kicked out of him, maybe worse. I'm glad he's gone. I hated having him around reminding me what love isn't.

Kirkland and I are having the time of our lives. We're like a French movie, a black-and-white one, a sixties one and we wear macs and take walks in the rain, except we don't wear macs, but we did take a boat ride in the park once.

I decided to give Gramps a break. He's actually all right even though he choked Mick with a relish I found unnerving. He's certainly strong.

Nelly and Gramps are having a great time. They're always out taking trips, they certainly get on well and he loves her violin, no surprise there. He also met Kim but she doesn't like him. She said, "There's something about him I don't like." I must admit Kim's pretty insightful about these things so I took it on board, though it's hard to figure out what the hell could be wrong with the saintly Robert T. Macdonald these days, he gives goodness a new dimension. He took in Sandy and gave him a trade and got him off smack, he can't walk past a beggar without throwing a few coins at them, and when he speaks of Lennie he only has the best things to say. I've drawn back from church visits, however, but Nelly goes every Sunday, he even has her playing while everyone gets themselves seated and comfy for the word of God.

Only problem we're having at the moment is Lennie. He's a bit of a growler right now and obviously has no time for Robert T. Macdonald, which is a shame 'cause Gramps really likes him. I'm kind of disappointed to be honest; I thought Lennie was better than that, but what a sulker. We all had a roast together last Sunday, as tradition commands. We'd been out with Gramps in the city, buying a few clothes; he's a very generous guy, like super-generous. He took me to Topshop and he got Nelly all these DVDs with Bette Davis, like a library of them, which we're going to watch together with popcorn next weekend at his house, an official sleepover. I guess it's time to check his place out and I've been promising for weeks. He was so pleased. Anyway dinner was a disaster, Lennie brought out wine and Gramps said he didn't drink, a lie, because he took us out to a restaurant recently and ordered himself a glass of red. He said so long as you were drinking wine with a decent meal then it was okay, it's when you're drinking it in a park with reprobates it's a problem.

Gramps has also taken over the rent of our house for when Izzy gets back. I feel bad about that 'cause there is no Izzy. I wonder a lot if Nelly wants to tell him the truth. They're so tight right now. He's so kind to us and sometimes it feels like we're thieves taking so much from him and calling him Gramps when we know his daughter is buried in the garden. We're afraid of course because the question of her whereabouts is in his pending tray. Now he thinks they're in the country somewhere. And they are, just not where he thinks.

Nelly

Being with Gramps is so much fun and Lennie's being such a good sport about it all. He even invited Gramps to dinner last Sunday though Gramps was a little disapproving of Lennie's alcohol intake and even remarked upon it. I assured him Lennie was no drunk, but he said I've to keep an eye on it and I jolly well will, truth be told Lennie's been a little wobbly on his legs of late, almost collapsed in the supermarket last week. I suppose he's not as young as he likes to think and it's true, he does like at least two glasses on a Sunday. "It's not beef without a good glass of red," he says, but if he should hurt himself on account of it I'd never forgive myself. It was very good of Gramps to mention it at all, subtly of course and avoiding any kind of offense. Such good pals they've become, they get on like a house on fire. Of course I invite Lennie wherever we go, but he's so darn busy. He's actually a bit of a loner these days and likes his own company. I suppose it was like that for a long time before we barged into his world with all our needs and wants, he's such a good man, it must be quite a relief to have someone else to share the burden with and perhaps take us off his hands, not in a mean way but Lennie is rather old and he most likely wants his home back, have a quiet evening playing his piano without feeling obliged to duet with my violin. Maybe he'll bake again, not much of it going on at the moment. There's so much to do I suppose, our laundry and the mess we leave behind each morning, I never tidy my bed. He even irons our clothes, although not so much recently on account of the burned shirt incident. He'd left the iron on top of it while he had a cup of tea. He must be tired. We certainly have taken enough of his time, whereas Gramps is full of energy and has a place of his own. He has a large garden, lots of room for weekend stays. I've organized one for next weekend and won't Lennie be pleased about that. I can't think of anything I'd rather do, to have a family again and a real one. Gramps even has a car, a warm car he can pick us up in. I always envied the girls being picked up in cars. In rain or snow. Parents reaching for snacks from bags in the front seat. Polished girls happy to be going home to gently lit houses, warm houses, the smell of dinner making its way to dining room tables where they sit and enjoy home-cooked meals. Homes like Lennie's I suppose. I think Gramps must be terribly lonely. I suppose he's as much in need of family as we are. I know it's what he wants. To be with us until Izzy comes back, except Izzy isn't coming back. Not ever. Whatever shall we do?

Lennie

The cheek on this one, let me tell you. He invites himself to dinner and he sits across from me the whole time giving me the eye and then he pipes up, "Two glasses of wine, Lennie? We celebrating?" Who the bugger does he think he is and in my house telling me what to do and what to drink and all the time cracking jokes with his *grandchildren*, buying them with gifts and the things they're weak for. If only they knew the danger in him.

I never saw it coming. It's all "Gramps" this and "Gramps" that. They're like little strays when you think about it, being fed scraps from strangers' tables, and strays never leave after scraps, do they? They're always hanging around for the next fishbone. I never fed them scraps. I fed them love, I fed them things they needed and from the heart. Oh . . . I'm an arrogant old fool, maybe they're the ones who gave, feeding my loneliness and perhaps they've been burdened by it. A desperate old man on his own needing company and faking family for them. Pretending to be their grandfather, until this liar shows up. Perhaps they feel the need to move on and of course I'd let them go; I swear I would, Joseph, if only I knew he wouldn't hurt them and I don't know that. Truth is I don't know anything right now. I'm so confused.

Marnie

Kirkland never returns calls. It really bugs me, I mean he calls but not in response to any call I've made. It's all "When can we meet?" "When you coming round?" "I've been waiting hours." "Fuck's sake, Marnie, move your hole."

Seriously, he treats me like an unreliable friend instead of his girlfriend. He's also swallowing a lot of jellies and I don't know where he's getting them but it's not from me, Vlado's seen to that. He says it makes sex better, which doesn't make me feel great; I mean why can't I be enough? He also says it makes his art richer, although I haven't seen anything except his dick in his hands these last few weeks.

Anyway Gramps meets me after school the other day and wants to have dinner but I have to give him the bum's rush 'cause Lennie's made dinner and Gramps gets all angry at that, I mean really angry.

It was pissing with rain at the time and I don't know what it is about the rain but your stance changes and you crouch and suck your face in and watch your shoes slapping on the concrete and in my case wishing I hadn't left my fucking brolly at school. When it rains the world changes and people change, it's like there's a rain etiquette all of a sudden. Glasgow gets quiet in the rain, no one talks, everyone is just trying to escape the rush of water and looking about for shelter or places to kiss or talk, maybe fight, puke, or fuck. Some people like to snog in the rain, it's considered romantic, especially in cheesy movies, but to be honest if someone kissed me in the rain I'd think they were a bit affected. I suppose you can cry in the rain but what's the point, no one would notice, which is a good thing if you don't want anyone to see you crying and of course Gene Kelly says you can sing and dance in the rain, but I won't be doing that any day soon on account of not wanting to look like a giant knob.

Anyway Gramps goes all mental about Lennie's mince and potato dinner with crumble 'cause it's Tuesday and Lennie always makes crumble on a Tuesday. Gramps was fuming, that's when I notice he's wearing a denim jacket as if it's not raining at all and it's not like it just started raining, it had been pissing down for days, people were bobbing about in boats in some parts of the country. Also his hands aren't in his pockets, they're waving about and he's standing straight, not crouching and the rain it's like tracing his anger lines, his frustrations and I'd never seen that in wet weather before, to be honest I don't think I've even looked at someone in a storm, unless I was on a train and like everyone else had escaped the rain. Mostly when it rains you're running, but Gramps is standing like a priest at an altar ranting about Lennie.

"Who the fuck cares what that queer has on the table," he says. "I'm your grandfather. You can't keep staying at his place, you know. He's not family."

There were a lot of orders in his assertions, a lot of commands and I didn't rightly appreciate them, especially when my phone started to ring and he grabbed it like he owned it.

"Gimme that!" I yelled.

"It's Lennie," he says, looking at the screen and as calm as you like.

Then he hands the phone back like he hadn't done anything nuts and goes, "Why don't you invite him along?" and a lot more pleasantly than when he was going mental over me going to Lennie's for my tea.

"Naw," I say because I can't deal with the oppressive weather and Gramps's uncanny ability to possess the emotions of a drill sergeant while it pisses from the heavens.

He then says, "Fine. Do what you want. I'm done," and walks away. Doesn't run. Marches. Still no hands in the pockets. Couldn't believe it. Don't normal people run in the rain? Even abnormal people, most of them anyway, the only people I can think of who walk in the rain are tree huggers, bag ladies, and total psychos. I've also seen David Bowie in the rain but that was for a music video and it probably wasn't even real rain, also Kate Winslet in a bonnet but she earns millions of pounds so she can walk where the fuck she likes. For a minute I wondered should I chase the old guy but then I get a text from Kirkland and decide not to. Gramps totally weirded me out anyway and to be honest I'm getting the feeling Kim might be right; there is "something" about Gramps.

Nelly

I am at my wit's end. Marnie told me to hold my horses on an invite from Gramps. He wants to take us for the weekend to his house and Marnie feels we must exercise more caution when we're around him, if you can imagine such a thing. She's suddenly of the opinion there's something strange about a man who buys her lovely clothes and takes us nice places, who buys me Harry Potter figurines and at great expense I might add.

What's wrong with everyone? Must we mistrust every single person who crosses our path? Her complaint was pathetic. She said he wore inappropriate rain attire and that he's "a wee bit creepy." Lennie was delighted, which shocked me beyond belief. I thought Gramps and Lennie were getting on famously, shows you how two-faced Lennie can actually be. I'm dumbfounded. A man doesn't have a mac and suddenly he's a good-for-nothing blighter worthy of suspicion. Damn them both.

Gramps has obviously been sent to us by a heavenly angel to care for us. Why does Marnie never want the same things I do? I can't be with him without her, she knows that. I can't be anywhere without my sister. I shall plead with her. I shall plead with every ounce of my breath.

Marnie

D on't know how she talked me into it, a weekend away from Kirkland, but I didn't like the idea of her hanging with "Gramps" until I'd gotten to know him a little better. He'd certainly funked me out the other day grabbing at my phone and generally creeping me out in the rain and I really didn't appreciate the slagging he gave Lennie. Lennie's been good to us. We love him. He's been the only family we've known in a long time. Don't get me wrong, I know the same is true of "Gramps," but he's going to have to find a way to accept Lennie as an important part of our lives. Thing is, "Gramps" thinks Izzy and Gene are coming back and he's getting rid of Lennie in some way. But he's not. It's Lennie all the way for us and I am pretty sure when he accepts Izzy isn't returning to her two wee cherubs a nationwide search for his daughter will ensue. He's already raising his eyebrows at us, as if we know her whereabouts, like Lennie used to. He thinks she's in the country because Mick found the passports and he secretly thinks we know where. I suppose we do.

To be honest Izzy's delinquent parenting has been a fantastic excuse and I know it sounds sick but right now we need all the deflection we can find, it's not easy hiding decomposing parents in your backyard.

His house was big and brand-new with an undeniable smell

of nicotine. He smoked and pretended not to. The lie made me laugh, but only a little, he was obviously a hypocrite, but he's also a Christian and it's kind of the same thing. The windows were shiny with plastic frames, the floorboards blond. There was a skylight in the kitchen and there were three bedrooms, but one was for guests. Our room was unbelievable. It had hand-carved bunk beds with stars sculpted into the headboards. The walls were pink and painted with cartoon characters. There was a ballerina music box. A rocking chair with cushions to match the walls. Shelves full of books for kids, matching bedspreads, and a desk for me. Oak. Polished. Not pink. He clearly intended for us to stay with him one day and not just for the weekend. I wondered if the spare room was for Izzy. I felt bad for him then.

Later we watched a Bette Davis movie about this woman who's minging and then gets gorgeous for a boat trip. Then she meets the love of her life and they never get together. It was totally depressing but Nelly loved it. He got us tons of sweets. Pick and mix. Mars bars and Coke. Everything that's bad for you. Everyone went to bed around eleven after a depressing chat about Izzy's childhood, a world we know little of. It sort of hurt us to hear of it. The things she'd done as a kid and the places she'd been. He had a ton of memories and I think he thought they were cute, but they just made us sad. He talked about how smart Izzy was and how she was reading at three and counting at four. He told us about Izzy walking into doors because she had issues with her eyes. He told us of the time Izzy called some old man Santa because he was fat and had a beard. He told us about Izzy stealing her mum's wedding ring because she wanted to be married to her daddy. He said she buried it in the garden and it took them days to find it. There was another story about Izzy kicking the dentist when she came out of an anesthetic and another one when she ran away and was found under her bed with a packet of jelly babies.

"She hadn't gone anywhere." He laughed. "What do you think of that?" he bellowed.

His stories made me feel uncomfortable because he forgot to mention what Izzy might have been doing while he was getting drunk and smacking her.

Nelly on the other hand got emotional and started to cry. We had our own stories about Izzy and none of them were cute. We had stories about an addict who neglected her children and hated herself, mostly on account of the man who sat opposite us now, telling us stories about an adorable three-year-old who had confused an old man with Santa and lost a wedding ring in a garden. I wondered if it was fair to tell him who Izzy really was and then I didn't care. The fantasy had to end. Izzy had been a dreadful mother and wasn't coming back and he deserved to know that. After I was done with my version of Izzy and unleashed what was a demonic truth I lift my eyes to an old man with his head in his hands, but not crying or anything, just silent and mulling it all over. I told him as much as I could remember and it still wasn't enough for me. I could have spent a lifetime telling him what it was like to live with Izzy and Gene, but he wouldn't let me.

"Enough," he begged and rubbed his face in anguish.

"She's not coming back," I told him. "Her and Gene have Mick's money. They can't come back."

"Don't be stupid," he threatened and it was a threat, like don't say what I secretly know.

"Marnie's right," whispered Nelly. "Mother told me. She said she loved us, but couldn't stay. She said we could take care of ourselves because we were good girls, strong girls. She left on a Sunday morning."

These words were not lies. I knew that from looking at her. These were the words spoken to Nelly by Izzy when she left for the garden shed and words Nelly had kept secret from me.

"What does Lennie know?" he asked.

"Everything, old fellow," said Nelly.

"Stop talking like that!" he yelled.

"She cannae help it!" I raged.

He bit the corner of a nail and spat it on the floor. His face was red, he hadn't meant to hurt Nelly, he just hated that Lennie knew something he didn't.

And that's how we ended up in bed, with him sulking downstairs and pacing the carpet.

Later that night I crept out to the landing and watched him sitting alone in the living room. He was in a chair and wringing his hands. He was drinking whiskey and smoking a cigarette. He was being all the things we'd never seen before and it made me nervous. If only he'd stayed sober and been a father to Izzy she might have been a different person, but she wasn't a different person. She was Izzy and there was nothing to be done about it.

Nelly

Marnie took the bottom bunk; it was wider, condemning me to a night of ruddy turmoil on the top.

He didn't tell us to go to bed, it was Marnie who suggested we leave him alone to ponder the realities she had bestowed upon him and with no regard for how I might have felt about such confidences. Listening to Marnie's truths and the ease with which they fell from her lips I knew only panic. How I wish the conversation had stayed with my mother as he knew her. His regrets were no doubt awash with shame, for he knew himself to be responsible for much of the suffering my mother had beaten herself with over the years and I felt jolly well sorry for the chap. He'll stop looking for her now. I am sure of it. He'll settle into a life with his grandchildren and together we'll find happiness. Perhaps Lennie could give up his home on Hazelhurst. We could live together. I'd hate to be without Lennie. He means the world to me. I wonder if I should mention it to Gramps? He does have three bedrooms after all.

Marnie

I was thirsty and so I went to the kitchen for a glass of water. On the way back I saw the light had been left on in the third bedroom and I went in to turn it off, a habit born of half-full electricity cards.

I noticed the drawer where the lamp sat hadn't been closed properly and I could see pictures and some private papers, someone had been looking at them and forgot to close the drawer right. I couldn't resist. It seemed Robert T. Macdonald had an entire life in there and wasn't that life half mine? I zipped through them, checking the door every five seconds. I didn't want to be caught snooping, though I was sure he was probably sound asleep.

I was stunned. There were pictures of Izzy as a child, loads of them. She'd been a lovely little girl and it made me sadder than Nelly's admission earlier in the evening. There was a picture of his wedding to my grandmother. How I wished for that dress and imagined it in a box in a dusty old attic carefully wrapped in tissue for my wedding day, but like everything else in our lives it had been lost in the hurricane that was our past, a past I'd never know, a past only hinted at in monochrome and nicotine-stained pictures. Mostly the pictures were of people I didn't recognize with random scribbling on the back. *Janet 1963. Mhari and Kip—Oban. Mum, Dad, and Wee Willie.* A picture of a soldier. Another wedding picture.

And then me.

In color.

With Izzy.

With Nelly.

The river rock wall. The climbing frame and there Nelly was pointing at something in the background.

Suddenly a hand placed itself on my shoulder. I dropped every picture I was holding except the Kodak.

"Love that picture," he said.

He looked hard.

"What is this?" I ask and throw the snap at him.

"You don't remember?"

I shook my head.

"She was running from your dad, on drugs, drinking. Listen to me, Marnie." He grabbed for my hand. I pulled it away. He looked angry.

"You turned us away?" I whispered.

He nodded.

"I was embarrassed," he says. "Ashamed. I was living in a wee town. I had a reputation; I was trying to start again. She was a reminder of things I just wasn't ready to confront so I gave her a little bit of money and she left. Then I moved and . . ."

"No forwarding address I suppose."

"I'm sorry."

"So what are you looking for now? You found Izzy already and then you let her go. You let us all go. Do you have any idea what we've been through? How you might have been able to help us? You abandoned her twice, how could you do that?"

He looked anxious, started biting his nails again.

"What do you want from us?" I asked.

"To make amends."

"No," she said. "It's too late for that."

I never even noticed her, but then that's how Nelly is. Quiet on her feet. Floating.

"Let me see," she demanded.

I hand her the picture. Her face hardens.

"What else is in there?" she asks.

"Just pictures," he said.

"Let me see," she says.

He's frozen. Can't move. Knows exactly what she'll find and he's afraid.

She rushes to the drawer, pulls out picture after picture and more than I had a chance to look at with him sneaking up on me. She finds photographs of a woman laughing and in a wedding dress.

"Who are these people?" she asks.

"That was my wife Brenda," he whispered. "We're broken up now. She wanted to open a bar and I'm not much of a drinker on account of God."

"And so you ran away," she mocked.

"I left."

"You're a bugger," she whispered. "A rotter, a cad, a good-for-nothing," she cried.

"Don't say that," he begged.

"I'll say what I jolly well please. Come, Marnie. We're leaving." Nelly wept.

"Not tonight. You can leave in the morning."

"I want to leave now," she said.

"And I said in the morning!" he sniped.

"Marnie. We have bags to pack." And she wasn't joking. She really packed those bags, including mine. I didn't know where to start. I didn't sleep a wink and neither did she and as soon as the sun rose we were out the door. He offered us a lift but we refused.

"I never want to set eyes on you again," she told him and marched herself to the train station. I followed suit.

Nelly

Jolly early it was, around seven in the morning, but wasn't he glad to see us. He looked tired, like he hadn't really been asleep at all and he took a long time to answer the doorbell. He'd been sleeping on the sofa and with the television on, which is very bad for his back. I shall mention it later. I didn't expect him to weep on our arrival, but I did expect shortbread and a nice cup of tea.

"Fetch us a brew, old man," I said.

"Coming right up, my love," and then we hugged. How glad I was to be home. How glad Marnie was.

Marnie

When I saw Gene walk out the door he had his back to me. Izzy was on the sofa crying and drinking. I didn't ask why. I had things to do and I didn't care. She was always crying and drinking. Gene had his music strapped to his ears. He was wearing aftershave, it smelled like gin. He finished off a can of beer and left it next to the telephone, then he grabbed a brown paper bag of vodka to drink on the road. He opened the door and left, and that was that. I didn't even say good-bye, neither did he. No reason. We just never said it in our house. People just left, except Nelly, she's the kind to say good-bye, would say it to her shadow. "Farewell," she'd have said or "Toodle-oo." Always made us laugh. He wouldn't even have heard her.

Feels like he's just disappeared and not dead at all although I did see him dead, wrapped in a stained blanket, being pushed into a shallow grave, his face disappearing as I threw gravel upon his eyes still open and still staring. Except they weren't, Izzy had closed them, this is just how I remember it.

I wish I had said good-bye to him. I wish I'd said good-bye to Kirkland, but I didn't get a chance. He let her scream at me and he let her blame me.

"How dare you come to my home?"

"I've come to see Kirkland, what's the matter?" I ask.

"Drugs is the matter. He's up to his nipples in temazepam, you little bitch."

"S'not my fault," I whimpered.

"Really? So you didn't know?"

I reddened, maybe it was my fault.

"Kirkland, tell her."

He appeared from behind her in a cloud of misery and wouldn't even look at me.

"There's no point, Marnie. Just go."

"She can't tell us what to do."

"I think you'll find I can. You come round here again, madam, and I'm calling the police. Understand?"

"Fuck you!" I screamed at her.

"Don't, Marnie. She's right. I can't see you anymore. I need to get better. We can't be hanging anymore. Just go."

She slammed the door, leaving me alone in bad weather and crying on his doorstep. When I looked up at the house I looked for him to appear at the window, to give me some indication everything had been for her benefit and we were going to be okay, but Kirkland was closing the curtains. It was over and he didn't even care.

I still have his iPod and his music, his compilations and his stupid love songs, his want songs and fuck songs. I should bin them and hate them, but I can't. I want to hear them and cry with them, I want to remember with them. It's too hard to forget.

Lennie

A tall dark stranger, just like the fortune-tellers tell you. His name is Vlado and he had a soaking wet teenager in his arms. Marnie had a boyfriend it seems and they'd broken up. She won't go into any details but was found by Vlado while he was jogging in Kelvinside Park, practically catatonic she was. Nelly's been tending to her ever since. She's a regular wee nurse and very interested in everything Vlado knows. He's a tutor of the sciences and he has been helping Marnie with her studies. Poor Marnie, she seems without hope at the moment, stares into nowhere and no smoking or drinking, and no eating. Very worrying.

Vlado didn't realize how Marnie's been living or what the girl's story was. He didn't even know who Nelly was, or me. Not half as sad as his story though. A daughter shot down by a sniper going to school, a wife in Switzerland who wants a divorce, and parents who died before the war. All alone he is now, but thank God he was in the park. He carried Marnie all the way home.

It turns out she's been cleaning his house, although he doesn't strike me as the type needing a cleaner. Marnie probably reminds him of his daughter and he wants to help her, she's certainly in need of it.

And what a rapport he has with Nelly. Every time she spoke

he smiled. She knows how to be a child that one and in the funniest of ways. I think he enjoyed it. I know she did.

Robert T. Macdonald is at his workshop right now and keeping a very low profile. The girls are so angry at him. It's hard to say where they'll find forgiveness. I couldn't believe it when they told me what he'd done, that he'd found his daughter already or rather she had found him many years ago and he'd turned her away and with two little babies to care for. Shame on him. What he wants now I can't begin to imagine.

I don't know what's coming for us all now. Sadness keeps me awake. It feels like there's rotten fruit inside my head.

Hope Marnie comes down soon. She's still upstairs listening to her iPod and very loudly. An awful buzzing of words at her ears, stinging songs about people who never die. It's not healthy for a girl. It's not healthy at all.

Nelly

Who is Kirkland Milligan anyway? A blaggard is who! My goodness the strangers she knows. The mind boggles with it.

I have tended her needs well over a week now. A broken heart is no laughing matter I expect. I have fed her soup, chicken procured by my own hand I may add. How she dribbles. I combed her hair later. Washed her face. All from her little bed.

Then I sang to her a Nana Lou song. Not so much as a paltry smile. Ungrateful wretch. I was done then, especially when she reached for the maudlin music she so loves.

"Oh pull yourself together, would you? I think I've killed Lennie's dog."

That certainly ruffled her feathers. Threw her beloved iPod at me, but what could I do, the dog was eating our mother and father. Intolerable fellow.

Marnie

She said she'd killed Lennie's dog but she'd done no such thing. She'd accidentally hit him with a small plank. She said he had been messing around at the flower beds again and she was trying to shoo him away. Luckily Lennie thought it was the thugs who graffiti his walls. Poor Bobby had a bandage around his head for days.

"I picked up a small plank of wood with the intention of waving him away with it, but he jumped up on me and I unintentionally smacked the top of his head. He really is a bothersome mutt, Marnie. Whatever shall we do about him?"

"Well, we can't murder him, can we. Lennie loves him," I remind her.

"Then what are we supposed to do? The matter is pressing." She moans.

"I don't know!" I yell.

"Hardly a solution, is it?" she says.

"Then, well, we'll have to figure it out, won't we?"

I underline *we* because I'm sick of being Wonder Woman for her. I'm too tired to save the day and it wouldn't hurt her to step up to the plate once in a while. It can't always be me. I don't want it to be me.

Nelly

How cross Marnie was with me and how relieved she looked when Bobby returned through the dog flap in the kitchen.

"Where have you been?" asked Lennie, hugging and patting him. "Oh my, what happened to your head?"

The dog just wagged his tail, his face dark with dirt. I knew exactly where the little devil had been and it was making me sick with worry. He gave me a look then and I truly felt and feel the little blighter knows exactly what's going on and means to get us caught. I'm thinking poison now. I have to do something to be rid of him or discovery is a matter of time. We've been through so much, Marnie and me, and to have it suddenly sabotaged by a mutt named Bobby would be altogether tragic. I can't have it. I won't have it. Our life must play on, our life must be protected and if Marnie won't step up then I suppose it falls to me.

Lennie

I was glad Marnie came to me and I'm glad I could be of some use to her. We went to the garden and drank tea and I made sure not to flinch too much when she had her cigarette, though I wish she wouldn't, they're very bad for the lungs, aren't they?

She wanted to know all about you, didn't she.

"How did you meet him?" she asks.

"With the greatest of difficulty. I was a music teacher. He taught English. He also had a girlfriend called Sadie. A right bag."

"What happened to Sadie?" She laughed.

"I couldn't care less," I said, the jealousy still ripe in my voice.

"So he was bi?"

"No, he was scared. We'd been caught kissing or rather I was caught kissing him. It's how we played it, no point in us both losing our jobs. Anyway the rumors about us were rife and he couldn't handle it and so he reached for Sadie. He almost married her, but she bottled out. Even Sadie knew he was gay."

"Doesn't matter, you ended up together anyway."

"Or I ended up with him." I laughed. "But it wasn't easy. Loving him was hard. Doors had to be locked and the lies had to be told, but still, it was a beautiful torment."

"I wish I'd never met Kirkland. I wish I'd followed my instincts and told him to fuck off, but he was so nice to me."

"Like Mick?"

"Not like Mick, different from Mick."

"Marnie, you don't have to love everyone who's nice to you. People should be nice to each other."

We played a little Scrabble after that. She's very good at Scrabble, but she kept chewing on her hair and when I told her to stop she twirled it around her finger instead. A very fidgety girl, always scratching at her knees or rubbing at her nose. Nerves most like, but when she won, oh my goodness. She jumped from the chair, and raised her hands up in the air and yelled, "Champion!" It made me laugh out loud, and so we played again. How she loves to play, but then her face fell, a shadow sweeping across it and I wondered what was wrong. She was looking at the floor and as I chased her gaze I saw what she saw. I was surrounded in a puddle of urine.

I'd pissed myself.

Nelly

I miss my sister. I miss her strength. There is something lacking in her of late and I am rather forced to take the lead in our lives, which I'm not at all comfortable about. It's simply not my place and occupies a great deal of one's time.

Robert T. Macdonald is a man who's not going to go away by himself. He is a phone call we won't take and a letter we won't read but he is persistent. We need to send a clearer message to him, but you try telling Marnie that, she's simply burying her head in the sand. I have seen him linger outside our home and outside our school looking for a way back. He is incorrigible. I wonder often why he hasn't just contacted the authorities and forced us to come and live with him in his daughter's absence. Perhaps he has fears of his own.

Vlado is an interesting character; one might even describe him as dashing. He certainly came to Marnie's rescue. It seems he is a teacher and has been giving Marnie support in her studies. Regardless, she needs to pep up and look lively. She has exams to be getting on with and our backs to watch, for Robert T. Macdonald isn't leaving any day soon. He wants much from us. I have seen it in his eyes and he won't rest until we are caught in the web he calls home. We must have a plan for all eventualities and if need be we must be ready to run.

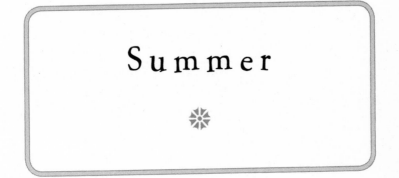

Summer

Marnie

Exams. Three thousand of them and Kirkland sitting in my head the whole time, a sort of gothic cupid with a joint in his hand instead of a bow.

Talk about a stressful start to the summer. Robert T. Macdonald is a pebble throw away from fucking everything up and I don't know why he's not calling my bluff. Maybe he likes his fish caught without a rod. I don't know, but it's freaking me out. And poor Lennie. Aging before my eyes. I couldn't believe it when he pissed himself. He didn't even feel it. It makes me worried for him. I told him to go and see a doctor, but this seemed to irritate him. He was obviously embarrassed. I know I was.

Thank God Lorna and Kim are done with, that's one duet I can live without, they're a nightmare together, but poor Kim, she's devastated. I could do without her leaning on Susie though. I've had a thousand texts from Susie begging forgiveness. I ignore her. We're done. I don't want to look at her ever again. Kim keeps saying she doesn't want to get in the middle of it all, as if we had a fight about lipstick or something.

"She was shagging my dad for fuck sake."

"I know but she's really sorry about it. Hates him like anything now. Where do you think he's gone by the way?" she asks.

"Who wants to know?" I scream.

"I was just asking."

I shouldn't have yelled at her like that, but I'm getting really sick of that question. It's not like anyone gave a flying fuck when we were stuck at home without electricity waiting for Tom and Jerry to waltz in with a couple of fish suppers. We could spend days without knowing where they were. No questions asked then, but now, it's like they're being head-hunted for a fucking job.

I've been through so much these last few weeks and everyone's been really good to me I know that. Nelly pours me baths and at night she comes into bed with me when I'm half asleep and strokes my hair. Vlado comes every night to go over my answers in the exams. He says I've done well, maybe a B in chemistry, which pissed me off a little. He reckons I "whipped the ass" in biology and that art history was a waste of time. He says with good grades anything is possible, but with my attitude Vlado reckons opportunity might be snatched from me.

"Everything must shift in here, or life will eat you up," he says and thumps his heart.

He should know, grieving for a dead daughter, missing a wife he will love forever, a wife who doesn't want him anymore and who's living with a heart surgeon in Zurich while he's stuck here supplying. In a way he's been the bane of my life. Drugs deadened Kirkland and tore us apart. I should blame Vlado but I don't. I should hate him but I don't. Truth is I don't hate anyone. Just me. Only me.

Nelly

Outrageous the cad should approach her at all given what he's put her through, but approach her he did and in a shabby black jacket. Quite the tom. They took a seat on the swings while I was exiled to the roundabout. Not a keeper this one, I can tell.

He takes her hand, she holds it. He reaches across and finds her lips. I don't know how she can, but it seems they'll never stop. She plays with his hair. They move from the swings. They hold one another and kiss again. He whispers to her. She stops in her tracks. She shakes her head and pushes him away. He swears at her. She walks away, he pulls her back. She runs to me and trips, she falls. I run to her, reach for her, the cut is bad. He comes toward us.

"Oh God, Marnie, I'm sorry."

He's on the ground next to her, the blood pouring from her knee seeming worse because of the confounded rain and not a brolly between us. It's always raining here. Raining and pouring.

A blaggard he is. A blaggard.

He grabs her face. "The jellies aren't about you. I'll get better, I just need a few. Speak to Mick."

She pulls away. "Leave me alone," she whispers.

We limp home in the rain, it didn't stop for almost a week if memory serves.

Silly boy. All this over a few sweets.

Marnie

I wanted Kirkland to mean it and when I knew he didn't I still wanted to give in to it, I thought if I had five more minutes with him it would be enough to change everything, but nothing would have changed and if Izzy and Gene taught me anything it was to recognize poison when you see it, but still, I was drawn to the weakness in him and kissed him. It was the last kiss, I didn't know that then, no one knows when it's their last kiss with someone who wants to leave them and if you asked them now, years later, they probably wouldn't even remember, unless they were one of those saddos who asked for one. Watching Nelly on the roundabout made me feel stupid for wanting to taste him again but he seemed stronger than before, although it was a lie. When he finally asked for his prescription I felt bad for letting Nelly's chicken soup down. She'd tried so hard to protect me from this. Of course every girl wishes she could be one of those pop star babes who wave their hands in the air yelling about being survivors but when love sits on one side of you and loneliness on the other, it's hard to stop the touching and the kissing. I suppose this is what it means when it's over, when you don't want it to be and when you want to start from the beginning and make it all right again.

At least I walked away. Don't know how, but I did, maybe because Nelly was waiting for me, I couldn't exactly leave her in the park, could I? Of course maybe she was the one who couldn't leave me in the park. She's become quite the grown-up recently. I'm glad for it.

Despite the rain we were home in no time. I had a scraped knee and wet hair. I also had Lennie asking where the hell we'd been.

"It's movie night," he says. And it was. He'd made popcorn.

Nelly

One feels quite at home wandering across the marble flooring of the Mitchell Library. If you didn't know where you were going you could get quite lost in such an ornate building, but I do know where I am going, I am going everywhere and can spend hours waltzing from one place to another. I have no particular destination in mind, I may pick up a newspaper in one room, I may seek out the past in another. I feel at ease in the library.

Except today.

I smelled him first, a souring odor of sneaky cigarettes amidst woodchip and oak. I couldn't believe he'd found me and in the most precious of places. Obviously there was no running to be done, not here and most certainly no shouting. There was just Robert T. Macdonald and myself.

"What are you doing here, you scoundrel?"

I closed my book while a fellow reader looked up from his paper, annoyance in his eyes.

"I want to go and find her," he said suddenly. "And I want you to come with me."

"Outside," I whispered.

My heart was beating fast. He was closing in on us. I could feel it.

"I will do no such thing," I told him.

"Why?" he asked.

I had to find an answer. Any answer.

"Because I don't care where she is," I spluttered.

"Speak to Marnie. I think the both of you should come. We'll find her together. I know we will."

He seemed desperate.

"I'm going home," I told him. I had to escape him.

"Home? To Lennie the Queer. I don't know how you can. The Bible says it's wrong."

"I will thank you to keep such remarks to oneself," I whisper.

"If I can't find my daughter then things are going to change around here. So you better get your suitcase handy. I'm done chasing you around the block, and that goes for your sister too."

He walked away, leaving me alone on the staircase, and I must admit I was rather afraid.

Marnie

Vlado suggests a bike run. "It will keep you fit and focused," he says.

In other words it will take my mind off Kirkland. I say okay and take Gene's bike. Hard to imagine he had a bike, but not hard to imagine he stole it.

It's a hot summer's day so no one's out looking for trouble, just some sunshine, maybe a wee tan, which usually turns red and reaches the front cover of the *Daily Record* with a shocker headline about burned skin, sometimes cancer. Riding past on your bike boys will give you the once-over and someone might whistle, but mostly no one cares about a girl riding her bike, it's too hot, they just want to be still and bask a little. They want to stretch out on the grass and listen to some music. They want to pull out the paddling pools for the weans and sit with their babies and their girlfriends and some want to do their washing, but mostly they want to love. Snogging and sunshine go hand in hand in good weather, so does shagging under a blanket and come winter there will be a lot of lassies with big bellies. Glaswegians don't need the darkness of a nightclub to live it up or get it up; consequences are words for teachers and lawyers, sometimes judges.

Fish suppers and ice cream do well on a day like this and if you're really posh a barbecue. Gene tried to do it once and almost burned the house down. I've never had a real one but I hear they're fantastic. Lennie is doing one tonight. I can't wait.

Eventually we reach the pub and Vlado gets me a Coke. He gets himself a Guinness of which he knows an abundance of facts having traveled as far as Dublin.

He wants to talk to me about something serious I can tell, but he stops himself and instead talks of his daughter.

"Sabina liked to cycle, you know this?"

"All girls like to. It's good for the bum."

He laughs.

Sitting on the grass the women around me stare. They assume we are father and daughter. I feel proud and want it to be so.

"She cycled all over the place," he continues. "Even when she was small, I remember her little legs pushing fast the pedals and all over the house, scraping on the floors, bumping into walls. She would yell for me to push her sometimes, she would want to be pushed fast all day long, but it was too much and I would say, 'No, Sabina. Enough,' and she would cry. When a child dies it takes a long time to remember all the good things you did for them. Sometimes I think if she had cycled to school that day she would have been too fast for the bullet, but I walked to appease my wife, to assure her it was safe when it wasn't."

I don't say anything. It was a lot to take in.

"You have no words of comfort?"

"I don't know what to say."

"Then this I take."

"Is there anything about me that reminds you of Sabina?"

I redden.

217

"You would be the same age."

"Is this why you want to save me?"

"I want to help you, teach you. I am a teacher. I was a teacher."

"Then why are you selling drugs?"

"They won't let me teach and I won't beg."

"You know the kids you want to teach, they get the drugs you supplied to Mick. They're like Sabina."

"They are nothing like my Sabina. My girl came from good home. She cared for herself, we cared for her. She did good in school and had never been kissed. She liked to pretend she had a horse, girls in this country they want to pretend they are forty."

"Addiction is arbitrary. There are tons of junkies that come from good homes. You can color it any way you like. You supply drugs and it's wrong, and worse than that you know it's wrong."

"I want to live, what do you want from me?" he snaps.

"I want to live too," I tell him.

"The Russians they have a saying: 'The future belongs to him who knows how to wait!' Why won't you wait?"

"There's no waiting here, only surviving. You think I didn't want a childhood?"

"And so you fly from it with the speed of a little bee in your tiny golden pumps." He was laughing at me again.

"They're the fashion," I tell him. "Everyone's wearing them. Not that you'd know anything about it in your cowboy boots."

"Let's go," he says.

We ride fast on the way back and it creates a perfect breeze. It makes us laugh, we can't help it. He looks back at me and tells me to catch up. I feel bad we talked like we did but a smile from Vlado reassures me that everything is going to be okay and I smile back.

Vlado stays for dinner and Lennie is delighted. It has been a great day and though I think of Kirkland from time to time, I almost forget there's an Izzy or a Gene.

After we've eaten, Vlado asks a sulky Nelly to play something, preferring a new energy to adorn the garden, and with Bach's help that's exactly what she does, albeit reluctantly, God only knows what's wrong with her now.

Lennie

He told her I was a queer and when she acted like she didn't know I have to say I was a little taken aback.

"You know about the boy in the park, don't you?"

She shrugged her shoulders.

"I know you know, Nelly," I whisper. "You've heard them shout in the night and you must have seen the graffiti on the door."

Her face went as red as beetroot.

"I made a mistake. A dreadful mistake and I can't undo it now. I wish to God I could. Do you understand?" I ask.

"I don't want to hear." She hushes me and puts her hands on her ears. I grab them from her head and grip tight.

"I am a man who likes other men. I like to be with them sexually and I like to be with them romantically and Joseph who lived here with me for so many years, you remember Joseph, don't you?"

She shakes her head and won't stop shaking it.

"He was my lover and when he died my heart was broken. My heart is still broken." I weep.

She is suddenly silent and I let her go. I am exhausted.

"I'm sorry, Lennie," she cries and we hold one another.

"It's okay," I tell her. "It's okay." I stroke her hair.

"I remember Joseph," she whispers. "I remember him, Lennie."

"Thank you," I say.

Marnie

It was raining hard when Robert T. Macdonald rolled down his window and told me to get into his car.

"You're soaked to the bone, lassie," he says.

"I don't care. I'd catch pneumonia before I'd sit next to you."

"That's not very nice," he remarks.

"You're not very nice," I remind him.

"It's not safe to be walking home on your own," he says.

"I know what you mean, all kinds of nut jobs spooking about." I say this and stare at him.

"I'll follow you in the car."

"I don't want you to follow me."

He ignores me and drives behind until I'm at Lennie's house. As soon as I'm inside, the mobile rings. It's Robert T. Macdonald. I send him to voice mail and then I listen to the message.

"Just checking to see you got home safely," he says and then click, he's gone.

When I tell Nelly she pales and tells me about the library. He wants all of us to go and look for Izzy. I make up my mind to go and talk to him. Nelly and I don't need to look for Izzy. We know exactly where she is.

Lennie

A foot and right under the dining room table. Bobby brought it in from the garden. Obviously I thought it was the bone I got him from the butcher the other day but on closer examination I could see it wasn't.

I didn't know what to do with it to be honest, I certainly didn't want it on any of my clean surfaces and so I put it on the sofa with the plastic covering.

When Vlado rings the doorbell looking for Marnie I think about chasing him but then I invite him in; I clearly need advice.

"You won't believe what the dog brought in," I say and take him to the sofa.

He comes in and of course he sees the foot.

"So, what do you think of that then?" I say.

"It is a foot," he says.

"I can see that," I say.

"Where did it come from?" he asks.

I shrug my shoulders. "The dog must have brought it in."

"Where is the dog?" asks Vlado.

"Out back."

We go to the garden and find Bobby sniffing at the flower beds with the lavender and running down the side of the girls' house, but this time he brings someone's limb. We can't decide if it's an arm or a leg. Further investigation is carried out and we find them. Izzy Macdonald and Eugene Doyle in a couple of shallow graves. I almost fainted.

"What have they done?" I gasp.

Vlado, as shocked as I am, sighs, and it's a mighty sound.

"I cannot be involved." He turns to leave.

"We have to help them," I say.

"No, you have to call the police. I cannot stay."

"But they'd get into so much trouble. And for these two shits it's hardly worth the bother."

He sighs again.

"Then what will we do, Lennie? Tell me," asks Vlado and with anger in his voice.

"Whatever we must," I reply.

Marnie

He was drunk and at the back of the bus, slurping booze from a brown paper bag.

"Marnie baby!" he yells.

"Sandy," I say.

"Cute dog," he goes.

"Thanks," I say.

Bobby's tail wags and his entire backside sways from left to right, causing a breeze of activity around my legs. I took him when Lennie wasn't looking and it was my intention to go as far as Drymen and let the dog go. He was constantly in our yard and it was making Nelly and me very nervous. We actually considered poisoning him, but he's such a sweet dog we couldn't bring ourselves to do it, losing him in the middle of nowhere was the only alternative.

"What happened to your face?" I ask Sandy. It was black and blue.

"Your grandpa threw me out on my ear, didn't he. Found out about my checkered past as a rent boy and told me to leave."

"You're kidding," I say.

"Wish I was." He takes another slug.

"Where you going to stay?" I ask.

"With my ma. She's impressed by my recent acquaintance with God and hopes to nurture it. It's a bed, isn't it?"

"I suppose," I say.

"So where you going with the dog?" he asks.

"Taking it for a walk."

"Where?" he asks.

"Drymen."

"Drymen's fucking miles away, Marnie."

"Thought he could do with a change of scenery."

That's when Bobby found his way to Sandy's legs. Bobby was all over him, and Sandy being Sandy liked it.

"Nice wee thing, isn't he?" he says.

"Yeah, he is." I give Bobby a wee pat and he licks my hand. I feel terrible about that because I know I'm about to lose him in the middle of nowhere.

"Want some of this?" Sandy asks Bobby, pouring booze into the cup of his hand.

"Don't, Sandy," I say.

"What you talking about?"

Bobby laps it up and I get the guilts, but then I think a drunken dog might be easier to lose than a sober one and he certainly liked the drink.

"All right," I say. "But just a wee bit."

Bobby drinks like a pro.

"Good boy," says Sandy.

"You're mad," I tell him.

He rings the bell. "This is my stop."

He finishes his bottle and then rolls it under the seat. It rattles from side to side. Then he smells his breath against the palm of his hand.

"Can you smell the drink off me?" he asks.

"A wee bit," I say. "Get some mints," I advise.

"I will," he agrees.

"Hope everything works out with your ma," I say.

"Hope so."

He pats Bobby. "Good luck, wee man," he says, and I feel bad again because I know I'm about to abandon Bobby in a place called Drymen and that's exactly what I do. Obviously I worried about what would happen to him. I worried he'd starve, but what could I do? There was too much at stake and he just wouldn't leave the garden alone. I had no choice and so I let him go and cried all the way home. I couldn't help it.

Lennie

Breakfast was quite the affair this morning. There were the usual requests for milk to be passed and Coke for cornflakes. Marnie also had a cup of tea and some toast, which I was very pleased about, I love to see the girl eat, but all the time I am thinking, *How on earth did your parents end up under the flower beds?* And you want to ask but you daren't.

"All right, Lennie?" says Marnie.

"Fine, love. And you?"

"No more than usual."

And there it was. Right there. I don't know how I could have missed it. Watching their earnest little faces digging into cereals and breads I return to the shadows they carry in their eyes and reflect on the long gazes they have shared, a gentle hand quietly urging silence upon a shoulder, a cough to interrupt a careless thought hastily replaced with another. I think of their walks by the sea, the quiet arguments and the uncomfortable glances across the dinner table. Mostly I think of them keeping this secret all this time and the burden they have walked with every single day since they have lived here. I think on the parents and wonder what on earth they could have done to end up dead and buried in their own garden but in my soul I know whatever it might have been, they deserved it.

I want to help the girls and I want to shout it out loud but as I am silent on the matter of my own grave I will be silent on the matter of the graves they have kept hidden in their garden.

Marnie

He was polishing the altar and arsing about with flower arrangements. I wanted it to be a quick trip so I didn't beat about the bush.

"If you want to go and look for Izzy that's fine but we're not coming with you. We don't care where she is. So leave us alone."

I turned on my heel, but as I'm walking away I can hear footsteps moving fast behind me, suddenly he has me by the shoulders and he's pushing me against the wall.

"Who the bloody hell do you think you are, little miss, eh? You think you can come in here and tell me what's what, you cheeky little . . ."

He loosens his grip, but my lips have whitened and I am visibly afraid.

"You don't decide anything from now on. I do."

He lets go of me and walks to the altar, he kneels and then crosses himself. In the name of the Father, the Son, and the Holy Ghost.

Lennie

The police found her in Vlado's apartment washing dishes. Turns out *he's* an illegal immigrant supplying drugs and perhaps responsible for the ice cream vendor's disappearance. I had no idea. Obviously they questioned her but realizing she was of little use to them they sent her on her way.

Of course I didn't expect Vlado to show up here. I gave him a right telling off.

"Selling drugs," I exclaimed.

"Supplying drugs," he said.

"And what difference does that make?"

He wasn't sure, I could tell from his face.

"I must live," he whispered.

"I'm disgusted," I told him.

"You are disgusted? A man who picks up boys in parks."

"He was a prostitute."

"And what difference does that make?"

Not a great deal, I realized.

"We are in this together," he reminded me. "You have forgotten what we have done?"

Of course I hadn't. We had come together for the girls. We had come together to protect them and that meant protecting Vlado and so I gave him whatever money I had on me, my car, and a place to hide.

Marnie will have a fit when she hears Vlado's gone. He meant the world to her. She loved him, but he can't stay.

I like to think I've helped these girls somewhat. I like to think they know it. It makes my conscience clean for all the wrongs I've done in this life, a little clean. Oh Joseph, God has punished me hard for what I've done in this world and for what I've loved and I fear hell more than any man I know.

Marnie

He left it on the fridge. My wages for the week and a letter telling me he'd fucked off, that's when the police arrived. They let me keep my salary but took the letter. Pigs are like that.

Dear Marnie

> *I have an emergency in my life and I must go.*
> *You are very young Marnie and it is precious to be young, it slips away from you soon enough and I wish not you should regret lost days, it brings many tears.*
> *Love to you Marnie, love to Nelly and all my respects to Lennie.*

Vlado

Another one for the absent people file. I'm going to run out of space soon.

Nelly

When Lennie poured a cup of tea last Wednesday he didn't stop when he got to the rim like a normal person might, he kept pouring until it was all over the table. One had to grab his hand.

"Oh my goodness, look what I've done here," he said.

I mean it's only tea good golly, but how he burns and loses things. I haven't had a decent meal in days.

Marnie

When I went back to his flat the door was open. The pigs hadn't even closed it behind them. The whole apartment was a tip. They had ripped it apart. Picture frames on the floor, books off the shelves, and dishes everywhere. I didn't know where to start and wondered why I was bothering. I suppose I hoped he'd be back or maybe I was looking for something to tell me where he went. Mostly I wanted to tell him I'd passed my exams. He definitely knew he was leaving because the picture frames were empty. Most of his clothes and a pair of tanned cowboy boots remained in the wardrobe. I felt bad for him then because he loved the tan ones, but it also meant he was wearing the black and I don't know why but it made me feel better knowing what he was wearing.

After I tidy up I empty the bins into the rubbish bags but when I get to the one by his bed I find it is full of crumpled papers. I open them up and discover they are various drafts of the letter he left for me. In one letter he wrote I reminded him of his daughter and he loved me very much. He decided against this draft and bounced it into the bin. In another draft he told me I was a "precious" and a "special" girl. He decided against this version also. He had written almost five different letters before deciding on the one he enclosed with my wages. All of them containing words like *character*, *beauty*, and *valu-*

able. I kept them all. I have them all. I search the flat desperately for a picture of Vlado and find nothing and it makes me sad because I never took any. I try to remember the last time I saw him and think of him on his bike by the Clyde laughing at nothing in particular. In my mind I snap this image and store it in my memory. It's where I keep everyone who's important to me.

Lennie

Tending your grave is no easy feat. I bring scissors and twine. A bucket and a trowel. I bring a bouquet for your birthday. I have purchased a plot by your side and will call you beloved on my gravestone.

I worry for the girls. My girls. I worry for their future, but I have stayed long enough and the gloom creeps closer. I have no fight in me anymore and I am weary, but I must remain able, the girls need me and there is much to put in place. I can only hope it is enough and that my girls can stay strong a little while longer. Courage is what is needed now, courage and stealth, for there is much to fight for and much to let go.

Marnie

Impossible to imagine that a man who liked women as Gene did should have adopted a taste for young girls. Even harder to imagine was Izzy loving a man like that, but she did, and when we were wee girls so did Nelly and I. How could we not? We were children, it's what we knew.

I remember one time coming home early from school a few weeks before Gene came into my room and I found them dancing. Izzy, slow. Gene, gentle. I suppose I was looking at the thing they were before the tearing, when she was a princess and he was a prince, defying the Furies to be together. Watching them love amidst the candles I could imagine the first moment their gaze fell upon each other and the first time they kissed. It made me understand their desperate clinging to one another. It also left me bitter being confronted by their love, for beyond it, the drugs and the hate and the infidelity, I saw an impossible reach for something else, something that had passed them. Until Gene died that is.

Thinking on Izzy clutching at Gene's cold dead body unlocked something inside me. A curiosity of sorts. I remember her breaking her heart, and though I despised her for it I couldn't quite fathom where this burst of love might have come from because she certainly didn't express such feelings while they lived. Remembering her grief I fully experienced what must have been an intense incomprehensible love once upon a time, but after years of abuse and hate how could she have summoned it to her side and so vehemently? Why had she summoned it? It was in that moment I realized the truth. Nelly had not suffocated Gene. Izzy had.

Lennie

He called at the other door looking for Marnie. He said he'd found her dog.

"That's not Marnie's dog, son," I told him. "That's my dog. My Bobby. Come on, boy." Bobby leaped at me and with so much gusto I thought he'd push me over.

"Is Marnie around?" the boy asked.

"Who wants to know?" I say.

"Sandy," he says.

He was a handsome lad about fifteen, red hair and blue eyes, maybe violet.

"I'm afraid not." I smiled. "Can I say who's calling?"

"*Sandy*," he said.

"You'll be looking for a reward, young man." I beam.

I was utterly delighted to have Bobby back and so I reach into my pocket and pull out a ten-pound note.

"S'okay," he says.

"I insist," I say.

He takes the money like a good lad and then walks away. I give him a wave for he was a very pleasant fellow. Very pleasant indeed.

Marnie

I have come here to our garden shed to ask you if you loved me as I must love you. I have come here to ask you why you allowed me to sleep by your feet and on your lap. I have come to ask you if there was love in your heart while you stroked my hair and when you moved me sleeping in your arms to a room never painted and to a bed never made.

I have come here to ask you, Mother, about the barest of larders and why you offered me coffee for lunch.

"We just don't have the money, love" is one answer.

I try not to think of you smoking cigarettes, or your wine-glass waving in the air when there was no milk or bread.

"Here's a pound, hen, take the bottles from under the sink and get yourself some chips."

Clanking down the street with four empties and a pound coin in my pocket makes me feel cared for. I'm thinking of those chips now and how they tasted to me, better than lamb or herbed chicken and not because I was hungry but because you gave me the money to buy them.

I have come here to ask you if you loved me and if you loved Nelly.

I have come here to ask.

I have come here.

Nelly

Sharon Henry wishes to be comrades of sorts. She is lonely and in need of companionship. She has friends of course but it's something deeper she seeks. She looks to be understood. I felt rather sorry for her and of course I have agreed to meet her after school on Friday. She has suggested we see a movie.

"Look nice," she tells me.

"Nice?" I ask.

"Make an effort," she says. "A bit of gloss maybe."

"But I don't have gloss," I tell her.

"Then borrow Marnie's," she says.

"Whatever for?" I ask.

"Because everyone wears it and it will make your lips look sexier."

"I couldn't give two hoots for what everyone else wears."

"Fine, don't wear it but at least wear something cool."

"What difference does it make what I wear? We're simply two chums going to see a movie. We don't need to spoil it with unreasonable demands."

"Okay, wear what you like, I have to go, meet me at the cinema at seven and don't be late," she commanded.

When I get home I discover from Marnie that Lennie set the kitchen on fire. He was making chips of all things and in the middle of the afternoon. He was in quite the state and apparently wandering around and telling the walls not to tell Joseph. Fortunately there wasn't too much damage and after a long nap he was back in the kitchen and cleaning the smoke from the walls. I have since checked the liquor cabinets for I fear Lennie's problems may originate from a more obvious source.

Marnie

Nelly thinks Lennie is an alcoholic. I think she might be right. He set the kitchen on fire and if it hadn't been for the very organized fire extinguisher he keeps under the sink I think the place would have gone up in flames. I'm starting to worry for the old guy. He clearly has a problem.

Lennie's phone rang tonight but there was nobody, except there was. It was Robert T. Macdonald, I'm sure of it.

Lennie

M ate," comes a voice.
"Yes," I say.

"You're trying to get into my car," says the voice.

"Are you sure?" I say.

"We've been neighbors two years and you don't know my fucking car. Give me a break."

"Then where is my car?" I ask.

"How the fuck am I supposed to know, but that one is definitely mine."

"Lennie?" comes another voice.

It's Marnie and someone else I can't quite place but she likes to whisper and if I reach far enough into my mind I can almost see her.

"Can we go home?" I ask them.

"Sure," says Marnie.

"Take my arm," says the other.

I take her arm.

"Good girl," I say. "Let's go inside and have some tea."

"Good idea," says Marnie.

"Where are my keys?" I say.

"At the end of your wrist," says Marnie.

I hand them to her. "Open the door," I say.

She opens the door. I find Nelly. I know Nelly.

"I think he's been drinking," Nelly says.

"I think you're right," Marnie whispers. "Let's put him to bed."

I am raised from the ground.

Jacket off. Shoes off. Watch on dresser. I fold into the duvet. A door is closed. I feel cold.

Nelly

It was a beastly evening. Sharon Henry is a deceptive way-ward type of a girl.

When I arrive at the cinema there are two chaps with her. Felix Murray and a brute called Sam, who I am given to understand is her boyfriend.

Pulling me to the side Sharon tells me I am to sit with Felix.

"Don't you fuck this up for me," she says. "I like Sam and Felix is a good guy. So be nice."

"Nice is as nice finds," I remind her.

"Felix is a wee ride. Every girl in school would crush their knickers to be here."

"I am not every girl in school," I remind her.

"No you're not." She sulked. "And what's with the violin?"

"I can't leave it at home."

"Why?"

"Because I won't."

"Oh whatever." She sighs.

Felix was quiet for most of the evening. He told me he enjoyed my violin performance at Christmas, which I very much appreciated. Felix it seems is the sporty type, he likes soccer and whatnot. It was a mortifying experience truth be told with Sharon and her beau clambering on top of one another like two dogs. A spectacle they made of themselves, even if it was in the darkness. Felix was a true gentleman of course and was respectful of the space I'd placed between us. He even gave me his jacket, for there is quite the chill in a movie theater. Later we went to a café. We have Coke and ice cream. We don't speak for a very long time.

"Where do you live?" he asks.

"Hazelhurst Road," I tell him.

"You like it there?" he asks.

"Very much," I reply.

"And your folks, what do they do?" he asks.

"I live with my grandfather," I tell him. "My parents are elsewhere," I say.

"Elsewhere?" he asks.

"My goodness the questions you ask," I snipe.

"I don't mean to pry, I'm just interested to know more about you."

"Whatever for?" I ask.

"Well I like you, don't I?"

"You don't have to," I tell him.

"No, I want to."

Sharon and her gentleman friend enter and making a colossal noise I may add.

"Hey, Nelly, play something on your violin," says Sam.

"I will do no such thing," I say.

Sam speaks to a waiter.

"My mate here can play the violin really good; can she play for five minutes?"

The waiter turns to a fat chap leaning over a counter and reading a newspaper.

"Hey, Willie, this girl here wants to play the violin."

"Aye awright," says Willie.

"I will not," I exclaim.

"Why?" says Sharon. "You're dead good and folk want to hear. Nothing wrong with that."

"Very well," I say and so I play.

As expected, the room goes silent and everyone is impressed. It's always the same. I often look to others while I play and can see a great deal from their faces. I see Sharon wishing to be anyone other than herself. I see Sam not caring about the violin at all, he just wanted to make me play and I see couples and groups of people all of them looking to share something special with one another, something to talk about and I see a lone soldier enjoying his coffee delighted to be surprised. I see Felix and the waiter and I see Willie grateful for the music and for a certain altering in his coffee shop. When I am finished everyone claps except Sam. Willie sends over four more Cokes. "On the house." He beams. We are a popular table and Sharon loves it.

"That was amazing." She smiles. "You're really good."

Felix nods. He's a quiet chap, Felix.

"So Nelly," Sam says, "your parents are on the dole, right?"

"Shut up, Sam," says Sharon.

"I just want to know how she's all posh and that. I mean she's fuck all like Marnie, is she? You adopted or something?"

I throw the Coke at him. I'd had enough of his tomfoolery.

"My sister and I are most certainly of the same blood. You blighter."

I am surprised when Sam starts to laugh. "She is fucking mental."

"Young man, I am leaving. Felix, it was a pleasure."

"Stay," begs Sam. "I'll get you another Coke. You can throw it at Sharon."

"No she can't," says Sharon.

Felix, a gentleman through and through, asks if he can walk me home.

"No thank you. I know my way from here."

"Nae luck, Felix," goads Sam, and I feel badly then. I did not mean to slight Felix in any way. He was a fine young man and kept his hands to himself. I don't know what I would have done if he hadn't.

"I suppose you can accompany me a little of the way," I tell Felix.

"Thanks." He beams and leaps to my side.

It is an awkward journey home and I am relieved he has something to say. He talks at length as regards his pursuits and plans for the future. He is not yet fifteen years of age and I wonder if I should have plans for my future. We decide to walk by the park. This is where he attempts to kiss me. I turn my head and give him a cheek. He seems disappointed. I suddenly kiss his cheek. He looks uncomfortable.

"Shall I play for you?" I suggest.

He shakes his head.

"No, that would be weird," he says.

He walks me as far as the bus stop on Byres Road. I have no intention of catching the bus, but I want to be rid of the chap and I imagine he feels the same.

"It was nice meeting you, Nelly," he says.

"You too," I say.

He hovers a little, as if he wants to say something else, but changes his mind and walks away with his hands in his pockets. I feel glad he's gone and then I feel sad, mostly for my violin. He said he liked to hear me play.

When I get home I want to speak with Marnie for I have a great many questions as regards the evening, but instead I find her holding up Lennie, who is as drunk as a skunk, and so we took him to his room before the neighbors were alerted.

Putting Lennie to bed was a lot like putting Father to bed and I can't deny feeling somewhat disappointed. Lennie is a man in his seventies and no spring chicken. It was utterly vexing. He's been an undoubted fool of late and I am thoroughly disgruntled. A beast he has unlocked within me and so I pull at his shoes and smack them to the floor. We did not remove his trousers. I left Marnie to remove his shirt. I couldn't face it. We did not steal his money either. He is not Father and doesn't deserve it.

Autumn

Marnie

It was the one place no one had looked. The garden shed. It wasn't even hidden. It was in a tool bag on a shelf next to tins of paint and broken flowerpots. A bag full of money. I wondered if Izzy had found it next to Gene's bed before she suffocated him. I wondered if Izzy had taken it with her to the shed before she hanged herself and then I didn't wonder at all. It was abandoned cash, and as far as I was concerned it belonged to me.

I decided to hide it at Lennie's. It would be safe at Lennie's. At first I hid it in the most obvious of locations, the attic, but then I worried I wouldn't be able to get to the attic in time if we had to make a quick break for it and so I hid it in the basement; this was a great hiding place, but again I worried about getting to it quickly and so I hid it in the wardrobe in the room Nelly sleeps in, but if Nelly found it I'd have to explain where it came from. It's actually difficult hiding bodies and money, but I was confident I'd find a solution, and after ruling out the attic, the basement, the wardrobes, the space under Lennie's bed, and the cupboard under the stairs where Lennie keeps an abundance of crap, I went back to the shed and put it on the shelf next to the tins of paint and broken flowerpots. It was the safest place.

After I hid the money I went back to Lennie's house only to be confronted by Susie hovering outside the front door.

"Hey Marnie," she says.

"Hey," I say back but with no enthusiasm.

"I'm sorry," she says.

"You should be," I say.

She offers me a fag but I say no.

"My nan says I can go to drama school, did Kim tell you?"

"I don't care," I tell her.

"So that's it," she says. "We're never going to be friends again?"

"I can't," I tell her.

"Your dad's a prick," she puffs.

"Hardly a news flash," I say.

"You don't know when he's coming back then?"

"Fuck off, Suzanne," I say and walk away.

I feel sad because I have lost a friend, I have lost Susie and I loved Susie.

Lennie

You have to have a light hand when making shortbread and use the very best of ingredients. I make mine by hand, although electric mixers are all the rage, aren't they? I keep my butter cold and blend it with flour and sugar with the ends of my fingers until it's like bread crumbs. Then I place it in a nine-inch cake tin with a removable bottom and press it into even layers before pricking the surface with the tines of a fork. I take a knife then and lightly score the top of the shortbread into wedges. I bake at 175°C for about forty-five minutes or until the shortbread colors, but ever so slightly. Finally I let it cool and remove it from the cake tin, cutting it carefully around the wedges and placing it on a wire rack. I sprinkle a little caster sugar for decoration.

Marnie

Kim and I had been out at the park having a laugh.

"Let's go back to Lennie's for some scran," she says.

When we get to the house I am introduced to Fiona Mullen, social worker extraordinaire, and she's ticking off Lennie for not letting the authorities know about the abandoned children next door. I tell the slag to piss off, which Lennie wholeheartedly approves of. I tell her she's got no right to barge in, when deep down we all know whoever holds the clipboard has all the right in the world. I don't say anything more, because I'm wondering where Nelly is.

She's a nasty bitch this Fiona Mullen and is unforgivably rude to Lennie, who quite rightly tells her to go fuck herself while reminding her there is no law prohibiting him from caring for two abandoned children, but this doesn't matter to her. He is deemed an inappropriate guardian, whereas my parents who neglected us every day of our waking lives were always deemed appropriate guardians on account of the DNA issue. No one wants to separate children from their parents, even when their parents are fucked-up delinquents.

Further to this, Fiona Mullen on account of Lennie's past feels entitled to waltz into Lennie's home and give him dirty looks.

I am glad when he tells her where to get off, I am glad he doesn't offer her tea or cake, but she doesn't care, nothing is going to stop Fiona Mullen yapping about the process Lennie should have followed when he became aware two minors had been left alone and took it upon himself to feed them and offer them shelter. That's when he tells her to get out. I mean really tells her. "Get the fuck out of my house!" he yells. It jolts because I don't think I ever heard Lennie swear the whole time I have known him, but when he starts to push the social worker out of the front door I know something is very wrong and not wanting him to get into any more trouble I tell him to calm down.

"I want her out of my home!" he yells.

"You better leave," Kim tells her.

"I have a court order; I don't have to go anywhere, young lady."

"Is that a fact?" says Kim, and with all the strength she has Kim shoves her out the door and locks it behind her.

"Push the table up against the door," says Lennie.

We don't hesitate, though we probably should have.

"Don't let them in!" cries Lennie. "Don't let them in."

He's running in circles and I wonder if he's drunk again.

"Check the back door," says Lennie suddenly.

Kim and I race to the only open door in the house and when we get there we find Robert T. Macdonald jumping the fence from our garden. We slam the door shut and look for things to jam it closed.

We hear sirens outside and looking around I can see windows that will be smashed and exits we will sooner or later have to walk through, but I don't care and that's when I remember the money I have hidden in the shed and wish I'd hidden in the attic. Then Nelly shows up all bleary eyed from the nap she was having upstairs.

"What the ruddy hell is going on?" she exclaims, because Nelly exclaims everything.

Nelly

The sound of sirens rouses me from sleep. Abominable. I peer through the window and see three police cars, scattered officers, and a woman with a clipboard. When Robert T. Macdonald comes into sight I know something awful is going on.

I am at the top of the stairs when I see Marnie, and she certainly looks harassed.

"What the ruddy hell is going on?" I ask.

"Lennie went off his rocker and locked the Social out," she replies.

"Lennie is under the influence of alcohol and in no fit state to lock anyone out of anywhere. Where is he?"

I continue down the stairs and find Kim playing with Bobby and drinking a bottle of beer while Lennie is in a tailspin over milk and tea.

It was a shambles. The neighbors were gathered around a yellow ribbon while Robert T. Macdonald shuffled next to a social worker. There were policemen wherever you looked, all of them trying to find a way into Lennie's house.

"Open up or we'll break through the door!" they yell.

Lennie hides behind the sofa.

"Gather yourself," I tell him.

"I will not," he replies.

"Open the door," I command the room. "There's no point to any of this."

Marnie appears from behind me.

"If we open the door, Robert T. Macdonald gets us. Is that what you want?" she says.

"Oh for heaven's sake. He's going to get us anyway. It's over. We can't stay in here forever. Sooner or later those doors will be opened. Don't be fools."

"She's right," says Lennie, who has suddenly composed himself into an apparent state of sobriety.

"Open the doors," he says dully.

Kim sighs. "Is that what you want, Marnie?" she asks.

Marnie shakes her head and then breaks down in tears. I am immediately displeased. She is utterly aggravating. I let Kim do the comforting. I have no patience for it.

"It won't be for long, Marnie," Kim says. "You'll be sixteen in December and you can go where you like then."

"What about Nelly?" she sobs.

"I can take care of myself," I remind her and aggressively so. I sometimes wonder where the girl's been this last year.

"You think so?" Kim mocks.

"I know so," I say and very firmly.

Without further ado the door is opened and Lennie is immediately approached by two policemen but instead of offering his wrists, he runs. I couldn't believe it. He jumps over the sofa followed by a very excited dog, throws himself through the back door and into his garden. "I am a murderer," he starts to yell, "I am a murderer!"

"He's drunk!" I yell out.

"Did you hear what I said, Robert T. Macdonald? She's

gone. Your precious Izzy. And he's gone, Gene Doyle, the most loathsome of the both of them. I killed them!" Lennie screams. He is on his knees, digging at his rosebushes; he is burrowing his hands into the dirt and pulling at it like a dog.

"Won't someone arrest me?" He laughs.

Robert T. Macdonald rushes to Lennie's side. He pulls at thorny rosebushes until his hands are thick with blood and earth. I am petrified while Marnie, her head in her hands, is stilled by dread.

"There's nothing here," cries Robert T. Macdonald.

"Dig deeper!" yells Lennie. "You'll find her." He laughs and gets to his feet. He is quickly handcuffed.

"At the bottom of *this* garden," Lennie announces to the yard, "I have two . . . two . . . two . . ." He trips on his words until he is lost to them and falls to the ground.

It is a ruddy mess and there is nothing we can do to remedy the situation. We are in shadow while our flesh creeps closer to the truth.

Someone yells for a doctor, someone calls for an ambulance, and then someone screams. It is Robert T. Macdonald and he's holding a skull. We don't know which one.

Marnie

Robert T. Macdonald paces the police corridors, all the time rubbing at his hands.

The police tell us Lennie has a brain tumor and will die. They question us about our parents and ask how long they've been missing. They try to make sense of the last nine months but we can't help them. The lies continue. It's what Lennie would have wanted.

"Confounded man," says Nelly.

"We knew he didn't like them but we didn't realize how much. He was always very nice to us," I say.

"He said he wanted to help us," says Nelly.

"Lennie fed us," I say.

"We thought they were in Turkey. Spain perhaps," says Nelly.

"We had no idea," I say.

"They were always abandoning us. It was their way," says Nelly.

"We didn't know."

"I'm not sure."

"We didn't know."

"I'm not sure."

"I didn't know."

"Good golly, we didn't know."

Eventually we convince them and we are released into the custody of Robert T. Macdonald. It's a really shitty day.

Nelly

I fear death, I have always feared death. It comes like a gale and never with permission. I would meet it again today.

It wasn't hard to get away. I said I needed the bathroom but this was simply a diversion, for I was out the door and on a bus to the Western Hospital within minutes. I felt bad leaving Marnie behind, but I had no choice. I needed to see my friend. He is my home.

Marnie

They weren't sure what happened to Gene and Izzy. Obviously we knew they'd been killed. Gene by Izzy's hand and Izzy by her own, but I suppose you can't tell that from a decomposed body after a while. I wondered if Vlado had been involved because Lennie would never have been able to move the bodies on his own. I hoped he had been. It was a weird kind of comfort imagining Vlado knowing the truth. I hated lying to him.

They decided Gene's body had been dragged through our house across our garden and into Lennie's garden. They also said Lennie's offer to help us in the absence of our parents was a manipulative ploy to cover his tracks, although someone else suggested he perhaps felt guilty. Nelly and I were the only ones who knew the truth. Lennie had saved us.

When it came down to it no one really cared why Lennie killed Izzy or Gene. Lennie was dying and there was nothing to be done about it. Robert T. Macdonald was livid; he sought justice and would never know it, and I was glad, he didn't deserve to know it. If Izzy's fate was the fault of anyone, it was his and deep down he knew it.

I cried when their bodies were discovered and not because I was relieved, although I was, I cried because I felt sad for Izzy and Gene. Even in death their lives were deemed worthless and it made me feel kind of worthless. They made me after all, and when I told Kim she went radge on me.

"You're the most valuable thing in my life and Nelly's. You talk shite like that again I'll smack you."

Kim's parents once again came to our rescue with the offer of a home, but the Social Work Department boked at the idea and decided Robert T. Macdonald, as a blood relative, would be a more suitable guardian. It didn't matter when we squawked about his violent past; it was the future everyone was focusing on. The past was dead.

Nelly

When I get to the hospital there's a damned police officer standing outside Lennie's room and good golly I didn't know what to do with myself and so I started to cry.

"What's up, hen?" said the officer.

"I must see the brute," I say.

"And who are you?"

"He murdered my parents," I whisper and not without shame. I felt discomfort whenever forced to blame Lennie for a crime I knew he had not committed. According to Marnie, Izzy was to blame, which was a relief because I always thought Marnie had carried out the unfortunate deed.

"He's conked out on the bed, sweetheart. No point," the officer tells me.

"I have things I simply *must* say to him. I shan't rest if I don't."

"Right," said the officer, a little baffled by the request.

"I beg of you," I say.

He looks around the corridor. It is empty and so he lets me into Lennie's room.

"Five minutes," he says.

"You're a sport," I tell him.

"That's right, hen. A sport."

Lennie

There is no drifting. I am weary and I am kicking. I see shadows and know voices. I feel strangers. They creep closer. I am lifted into foreign arms and taste ice cream. It is rich and it is warm. I am returned to the gloom and scream for the roses. I don't tell her she is safe. I don't say that it's over. I tell her something far. I tell her something hidden. I hope it finds her well. I ask for someone who is late and I hurt for the dog. I feel soft and glad. I feel ready and able. I think of you until the rainbow pales.

Marnie

She'd run off and Robert T. Macdonald was furious. He knew exactly where she'd gone and meant to drag her from his side. I spend the journey to the hospital convincing him she has Stockholm syndrome. He seems taken by the idea. When we get to the Western he instructs me to fetch her. He waits downstairs in the lobby.

"I'll kill him if I see him," he says.

I find her on a chair outside Lennie's room. She is eating crisps and sipping Coke. I expect to find her in hysterics but she's not. She's just chewing and slurping at her drink. It's annoying. I ask for Lennie and she says he's asleep. I say I want to see him and tell the officer I need to confront the man who murdered my parents, but I don't get a chance to confront Lennie about anything because the nurse in his room emerges and tells the policeman that Lennie has died.

Nelly

Birds keep chirping and music keeps playing. Life continues as another life ebbs away.

We have seen death before, Marnie and I, a mountain of ice melting over time, drops of water freezing at your core reminding you every day of that which has vanished, but the despair we know today is a sadness sailing sorrow through every bone and knuckle.

There is no moment in which we say good-bye, there is no finality as he slips into peacefulness, he simply leaves us, and though I seek courage when he passes I am weakened by tears, but I must hide them for he leaves us a lie to conceal, a lie he sent to save us.

Marnie

Their funeral was a joke and no expense spared. He had two cherrywood caskets with gold crosses carved onto the lids. Then he had them buried together and planned an ornate tombstone with words like *Beloved* and *Dearest* engraved on marble. I would have laughed, but I was too sad and not for Gene and Izzy, but for Lennie. His funeral had been the previous day. Kim went because I asked her to. At first she couldn't understand why I needed her to attend the funeral of the man who had murdered my parents but when I told her I needed closure she bought it and went along. She said the priest gave a brief Mass to an empty graveside. She said his coffin had one wreath of flowers. Nelly and I sent it anonymously—a circle of roses. She said there were no pallbearers and that strangers lowered him into the ground. She said she didn't stand by the grave and hid by the trees. She didn't want anyone to see her.

It wasn't fair we couldn't go to Lennie's grave but this is how it had to be and how Lennie himself wished it to be. Maybe one day when no one was looking we could stand by his tomb and thank him for all the wonderful things he had done for us but not on this day, on this day we were being forced to sit through the service of two parents who had neglected and abused us. It was sick.

Robert T. Macdonald said a few words mostly about himself and his regrets as a father. He went on about how he wished he had been there for his daughter and how he wished he had known Eugene. That made me laugh. Robert T. Macdonald would have flipped his lid if he'd known Gene. Susie was hysterical of course, it was nauseating. She suggested she sing a song, and Robert T. Macdonald allowed it. It was a beautiful song. It made me sick. Then he did a verse about death and how it was in the next room, I stopped listening around about then, the man was giving me the dry boke.

When we are finally moved into his home, it smells of bleach and reminds me of death. He is pleased to see Nelly and carries her violin case. He feigns a smile for me and carries nothing. He enthuses over the dog and gets down on his knees and practically snogs him. Bobby wags his tail and jumps all over him. They are immediate friends. The dog knows no loyalty. Robert T. Macdonald makes us something to eat, and though Nelly is hungry, I am not. He gives us a list of daily chores, they include laundry and hoovering and walking the dog. Nelly says nothing and helps herself to more of his lumpy custard. I shove my list to the side of my plate, wishing I could shove it somewhere else. I want to see Kim so badly but he says it is late and tells us we have school in the morning and we are sent to bed. Sent.

Nelly

Robert T. Macdonald cries in the nighttime. He cries for a daughter he'll never know and I feel rather badly for his tears. Marnie is without sympathy and I don't quite care for her attitude. His daughter was also our mother, was she not?

We are not to mention life on Hazelhurst, but Marnie insists we have possessions to retrieve from Lennie's home. Robert T. Macdonald is enraged and refuses.

"You are not to enter that monster's home, do you understand? I will replace whatever is needed. Clear?"

I am clear, Marnie is not. When she offers a "But . . ." he throws a glass at the wall.

"I said, *clear*?"

Marnie nods and then skulks from the room.

Truth be told I feel bothered he has called Lennie a monster and then I remember it is the cost of the new reality we are living: Lennie is a murderer and we are the innocent and orphaned.

"Apologies, Grandfather. Marnie isn't thinking as one should right now."

He tells me to make ready for dinner. We are having steak pies from a tin. I know it won't taste good and make plans to take over his kitchen.

"Perhaps I can help," I suggest.

"To do what?" he grumps.

"You have eggs?" I ask.

"Tons," he says.

"Then you are in good hands," I assure him.

We must move on and we must make this work. The past is the past and Robert T. Macdonald's regrets are tenfold. Whether she likes it or not he is our family and with a little cooperation from all of us it's possible we can all get along. It's imperative, for we have nowhere else to go.

Marnie

Every morning Robert T. Macdonald makes us tidy our beds and not like we used to by throwing our duvets on top, but with straight smooth angling. It's like living in a barracks.

I have porridge for breakfast. Nelly has her cornflakes and Coke. Television is limited to one hour and he makes us go to church every Sunday. We have to wear skirts, but when he sees my mini he has a fit and takes me to Oxfam where he buys me something long, flowery, and ugly. I hate him.

Nelly is quick to fall into line and is eager to please. It's like she's developed some kind of amnesia and forgotten what a nut her "gramps" actually is.

He gives Nelly the room he originally planned for Izzy and lets Nelly decorate it herself. He gives her money for whatever she wants while forcing me to live among the pinks and cartoon characters in a room he meant for both of us.

"It's best you have your own place," he tells Nelly. "Away from bad influences."

He says this good and loud and obviously for my benefit. I play deaf while Nelly doesn't even flinch. She's said nothing since we got here and it worries me.

A midnight escape to a nightclub ends in tears for me when I accidentally return through his bedroom window, falling on his head smelling of alcohol and fags. He goes crazy and pushes me to my knees and makes me say the Lord's Prayer at five in the morning. I am too drunk to refuse him, although I stutter over the part about "Forgive us our trespasses" because I went to a Protestant school and we say "Forgive us our debtors," so our words collide but he doesn't correct me and we get to Amen without too much fussing. The next morning I wake to hammering. He has put a lock on the outside of my door.

"You're going to sit in here for the rest of the day," he spits.

"No way," I say.

He went right up to my face then. "While you're in my house you're going to do as you're told, you nasty little witch."

"I'm nearly sixteen, you can't keep me here forever."

"But I don't want to keep you forever. I don't want to keep you at all." He laughed. "I can't wait till you're sixteen. Sooner you're out of your sister's life the better."

It was the one thing I hadn't considered: he didn't want me at all. He wanted Nelly, malleable and afraid. She was to be his family and as soon as he got the chance he was going to erase me.

Later that night Nelly came to the locked door.

"Please, Marnie," she whispers, "don't misbehave. He'll separate us for sure. I know he will. Do it for me. He's not as bad as you think."

Nelly working for Team Macdonald was more than I could handle and so I told her to fuck off and that's exactly what she did.

Nelly

Why must she be so difficult? It might not be much of a home, but it is better than no home and I am tired of running. If she'd only accept his ways, life would be so much easier. How he berated her for escaping and in the middle of the night and how he rages. He is a tempest in particular moods and knows no calm. I miss Lennie but I do my utmost not to compare them, sure it would lead to more misery, and so I try to fit into Gramps's world as best I can. I could be here a very long time, with or without Marnie. It's a dreadful state of affairs. If she could just toe the line and if not for herself, then for me. He's not so bad once you get used to him. He can be very accommodating so long as everything else is running as it should. Dinner eaten by 5:30. Homework finished by 6:30 and clothes ironed and ready for the following day by seven. Television till 7:30, bed and prayers at eight. Marnie cannot abide him. She's never done homework in her life, has never needed to do homework. As for her clothes he chooses what she wears, and you can only imagine his choices. Marnie keeps her clothes at Kim's and changes as soon as she gets to school. Gramps says Marnie's been running amok for too long now. Perhaps he is right. He says Marnie is a negative influence and will drag me down. He tells me how proud he is of my gifts and my manners.

"Could take you anywhere," he says.

Marnie is to be kept in a locked room for twenty-four hours or until she sees sense. I hope it's soon. I should go and speak to her.

Nelly

I take a walk in the park and meet a ghost, a vampire, and a witch. It is Halloween and I wish for a costume of my own. I remember how Mother loved this particular holiday and always in fishnet stockings. She was a cat one year, a nurse the next, and before she died an oversize schoolgirl. When we were little she always took us with her, but as we aged the celebrations and parties were mostly for her.

"You're too old to go trick-or-treating," she told us.

Marnie was ten and I was seven.

"Please," begged Marnie.

"No," she snapped.

For the rest of the evening we were tormented by revelers rapping on our door looking for treats. We turned the lights off and went to bed.

When I get to the house I find Gramps dressed as a clown. He treats children to toffee apples and sweets. He is kind and he is generous. I like this man and I think everything is going to be okay until a boy shows up with a pillowcase over his head. It is splattered with red ink, which I presume to be blood.

"What are you supposed to be?" asks Gramps.

"I'm a headless ghost," says the boy.

"I don't think so," says Gramps, closing the door.

"What about my sister?" asks the boy. At his feet stands a little fairy.

"Okay, one for her, but your costume is rubbish. How old are you anyway?"

"I'm ten."

"Ten," squawks Gramps. "You're too old to go trick-or-treating," he says. "Away you go."

The little girl takes her brother's hand and they leave without the toffee apple.

I go to my room and turn off the lights.

Winter

Marnie

When Robert T. Macdonald drops us at school I tell Nelly I have somewhere to go. She begs me to stay but I can't and since I'm not sure if I can trust her anymore, I don't tell her about the bag.

"He'll be so angry," she reminds me.

"So what," I say.

"He is unbearable when he's angry with you," she says.

"I take it by unbearable you mean a big fat psycho."

"Why can't you just try?" she screams.

"Try what?" I yell.

"Try to make this work. It's a home, isn't it?"

"He's mental. Don't you see that? We can't stay there. I can't."

"Well I have to. You think he'll let me see you if you leave?" she cries. "He's not so bad, Marnie."

"Oh my God. You think you're getting on with him when really you're just managing him. It was the same with Gene. You thought you could keep him away by being you and then you couldn't, neither of us could."

"Don't talk of such things."

"I'll talk about what I like."

She slaps me and I can't believe it. I think of slapping her back but I don't. I'm too shocked and I'm hurt. I'm so hurt.

"You fret too much," she whispers.

"Fuck you and your 'fret,'" I say. I turn to leave and she pulls me back.

"Please stay in school. If you would just try to do as he wishes."

"That's the thing, Nelly, what Robert T. Macdonald wishes is a little unclear to me right now and I'm not hanging around for it to be clarified."

I break away and leave her crying. I don't cry, but I know I wanted to.

Nelly

He follows her every move. I can see him. I do what I can to distract him but I am running out of music. He doesn't want her, I can feel it and I can't bear to think of a life without her for he will surely forbid any contact with her beyond her seventeenth year. Last week she played truant from school and a demon was unleashed, now he won't let her out of his sight and it is a miserable state of affairs. He kept her on her knees for at least two hours and how they bruised. I didn't know what to do for her and so I waited for him to go to the shops for his blasted lottery ticket and went straight to her room. I found her listening to her con-founded pop music, her head bobbing around like a ball on water. She wouldn't talk to me and I had to get through to her. I didn't know the song she was listening to at all, but it had a bizarre kind of energy and so I let my head dance with her head and before I knew it we were jumping on top of her bed. It was so much fun. We held hands and laughed, though I did feel badly for her knees. I didn't even hear him come in and he wasn't best pleased.

"Get off the bed," he snarled.

Marnie turned the music down.

"Go to your room," he said to me.

He sulked all through dinner and could barely look at me.

I asked if he'd like me to play and he reluctantly agreed. I chose a religious piece and it brightened him in no time.

"You'll always have a family in God, Nelly, and don't you forget it."

Marnie looked miserable. She hardly ate a thing. Her appetite is waning of late, which is a dreadful shame, for Lennie spent a great deal of time fattening her up.

Gramps has obviously forgotten I have a family in Marnie and I wonder then if my sister has also forgotten. I think perhaps she has. Lennie said she'd always need reminding. He told me a lot of things in the end, but one thing in particular and I mustn't forget it.

Marnie

Nelly was pissed off with me but what could I do? I had to get the bag. It's our only way out of here. He obviously went nuts but I didn't care. I'm too desperate to care. I'm not staying here and he's not taking my sister from me. He's already forbidden contact with my friends and when he says friends he means Kim.

His regime is a prison for me. Every day before school he makes me empty my pockets for fags and other contraband. He actually searches me like one of those people at airports looking for bombs in your handbag. Of course Kim has all my contraband. He takes us to school in his sad little Peugeot around 8:15 and we get there around 8:30, but then he makes us sit with him until the bell rings at nine. He watches as we enter the school gates and calls three times a day to ensure I am sitting in maths or English. He won't leave me alone.

I have barely said two words to Nelly in weeks. I feel so betrayed by her compliance.

At breakfast this morning he had us sing from hymn sheets, but Nelly wouldn't play. She said her neck hurt.

"Abide with me, fast falls the eventide,
The darkness deepens; Lord, with me abide.
When other helpers fail and comforts flee,
Help of the helpless, O abide with me.

"Swift to its close ebbs out life's little day,
Earth's joys grow dim, its glories pass away,
Change and decay in all around I see,
O Thou who changest not, abide with me.

"Come not in terrors, as the King of kings,
But kind and good, with healing in Thy wings . . ."

We have to get out of here.

Nelly

He slapped me. He waited until she wasn't looking and slapped me.

"When I ask you to play then that's exactly what I expect from you. You have a gift but it is God's gift and you are obliged to share it."

"Yes," I whisper.

He kisses my forehead and I don't cry.

When we drive to school everything is wet and gray. We pass tower blocks and cross motorways, nothing is warm. I watch him drive, his nose red and dripping from the rain, I watch Marnie fixated on her hair. I wonder about the vanished; about Mother and Father, about Grammy and Lennie. I try not to cry for them, I won't cry for them and so I reach for my book and read, I can't help it.

Marnie

I find her sulking in the cafeteria, gurgling milk like a little kid.

"All right?" I ask.

"What do you care?" she mumbles.

"I care a lot as a matter of fact."

"What do you want?" she says and then plays with her sandwich.

"I can't stay at *his* house," I tell her.

"I know," she says.

"So what do you think?" I ask.

"About what?" she says.

"About getting the fuck out of here," I say.

I expect resistance and fear. I expect excuses and reasons, what I don't expect are keys.

"Lennie's place in Firemore," she says. "You should leave as soon as you can."

"How long have you had these?"

"Lennie gave them to me."

"We could have left ages ago, Nelly."

"I want to stay. Give it a chance. Know some semblance of a family. I'm tired, Marnie. I'm so tired. I don't want to run."

She started to cry. I put my arm around her.

"You have a family. I'm your family."

"I thought you'd forgotten," she says.

"I won't let anything happen to you. I swear. I'd kill him first."

This certainly rattles her cage.

"Let's hope you don't have to."

I hope the same, but only a little bit.

Nelly

All she has is a set of keys. It's ruddy ridiculous. However will we survive without money? I don't think Marnie has thought this through at all. I held them back for this very reason, but there has been much in our lives Marnie has not thought through and oh my, the trouble we have known on account of it, it beggars belief.

I wonder if I can live without school and libraries. I wonder what I can take with me. She says the clothes on my back. I wonder if there are cornflakes and Coke. There is so much one needs, especially when embracing new environments. How I love the cottage, but does she expect us to live on fish and grass? She is sixteen in one month and assures me we will know all kinds of freedoms.

"I'm legally able to take care of us, Nelly. It'll be okay," she says. "Trust me."

No one is to know of our whereabouts, not even Kim.

"I don't need threads so you're not to talk to anyone. Do you understand?"

I can't imagine who she'd think I'd talk to, given I have no friends to speak of. I only have Marnie.

Marnie

This morning I shared a sneaky fag with Kim, it was to be our last and for a long time to come.

"You must be going mad in that fucker's house," she says.

"I am," I say.

She sighs for me.

"I couldn't do it, but I respect you can."

But I can't, Kim, is what I want to say. I'm leaving and won't be back for a while and I'm going to miss you like crazy, you mad bitch.

I say nothing and stub out my fag with the toe of my shoe. It's like a dance I do. Kim follows suit and we say our good-byes for the day. I want to pull her back and hug her, I want to tell her I love her, but I can't. It would make no sense and she'd know something was up. I decide to walk her to the bus stop, knowing I'll be late for Robert T. Macdonald but I don't care. When Kim gets on the bus she makes a face through the window and I give her the finger. That was our good-bye. Kim licking a window-pane and me pissing my hole laughing at her.

Later I sneak into the back of the theater where Susie is singing in the school play. I make sure no one can see me, especially Susie. I don't go for the whole performance; I just want to see her and hear her sing one more time. I deserve a song from her, even if it wasn't for me.

Nelly

There was no plan, we would simply leave in the night and catch a bus as far as Inverness. We were taking the dog. Marnie was reluctant but conceded it would have been Lennie's final wish that his Bobby stay with his girls, as opposed to a raving lunatic with a penchant for whiskey (and no glass according to Marnie).

I didn't pack much in my rucksack. They had to be small enough to fit under our beds. It wasn't a very big bag sadly and though I was able to squash a box of cornflakes into it and various undergarments, not to mention a few cans of Coke, Marnie was absolutely livid. She said they weren't essentials but I closed my ears and shook my head and not wanting to upset me any further she permitted me to take my nourishments, though she didn't talk to me for the rest of the day and complained of having to take extra things for me in her bag. What she didn't know is that I was also wearing five T-shirts and two jerseys. I was boiling.

Marnie

And so the rabid chitchat begins again. She wouldn't stop. "Where are we going? How will we get there? How much is a ticket? How long is the journey? What will we eat? Can you fish? Lennie said to stay away from the mushrooms. Do you know how to light a fire? How will we do laundry? What about electricity or is it gas he has? I can't remember. Do we have milk?"

I could have screamed, but not wanting to ruffle her feathers I find an answer for her every concern.

She wanted to take everything including the pillow Izzy had suffocated Gene with. Sick. I said no and she let it go. She wanted to take her cornflakes, however, and cans of Coke for her ridiculous cereal. I hope to God they'd be easy to locate in Firemore. She'll have a fit if all we have is porridge. It was a little bit of a setback the demand for cornflakes and Coke; I thought she was getting over these things. She seems to have slowed down in recent weeks, bordering on being normal to tell the truth, it must be the stress of running away fueling the nuttiness in her. Maybe it's time to tell her about the money.

Nelly

Marnie has a bag of money, all of it tainted with misery and other people's undoings. I don't want to take it and urge her to leave it behind. She uses expletives and I am without words.

"We won't survive without cash. Hard cash."

"It's not right, Marnie. It's not right," I tell her.

"What's not right?" she says.

"You know very well."

"Yes I know, but what do you know?"

"Nothing, nothing at all."

"You sure?" she says. "You can say it you know. *Drug money*. D-R-U-G-S."

"I don't want to know."

"You never want to know anything real, do you? And to think you were doing so well recently. Thought you were finally growing up."

"It's not right," I say.

"You know what's not right, starving. We have to take this money."

"I don't want to," I say.

"Think of it this way. This is every penny and every pound Izzy and Gene stole from us to buy drugs. We're just taking it back and with a little bit of interest. It's fair, Nelly."

"I'm not sure," I say.

"Think of what we can buy with this money. Safety and security. You want to send it back to the dealers to buy more drugs and hurt more people like you and me or do you want to take it and start a new life somewhere else?"

When she put it like that there was no arguing with her. Morally it is wrong but ethically it is correct and so the money comes with us and I've never seen so much of it in my life.

Marnie

We've come a long way, Nelly and I, but sometimes I forget what a giant fanny my sister can be. She wanted to leave the money behind. She wants to go to Firemore and catch fish and eat leaves. She wants to grow cucumbers and tomatoes and in these climates. She is the world's greatest plum. I want to slap her but I don't. I need her focused on getting out of here and not afraid of her sister smacking her face in.

Robert T. Macdonald continues to make my life hell and on our last weekend together he takes us to the cemetery where Izzy and Gene are buried. The tombstone is ready and he wants us to stand in front of it and cry. We are thinking of nothing except getting away. The tombstone is bullshit and implies Gene and Izzy were married. He even changes her name to Gene's name. It's so wrong. The marble tells the story of two people who are "Dearly missed," who are "Beloved" and who have been "Taken but not forgotten." I want to spit at it, just like they do in the movies. Nelly starts to cry but she's hushed by Robert T. Macdonald.

"No tears please. Just play something nice."

She doesn't want to but she has to and gives us a little Bach, but he hates it and asks her to choose something more celestial and so she plays "Amazing Grace" as best she can. He is close to tears and I realize he likes to grieve. This is a place where he can actually be a father to Izzy because all he has to do is show up with flowers and twine and when people pass him by and see him digging around the grave they won't know any difference. They'll glance across the tomb and feel pity for a man who lost his daughter three times and they really shouldn't.

Nelly

We crept slowly down the stairs and crossed the living room to the front door. Fortunately the stairs don't creak and so we were spared the amplified noises one imagines when one is making a break for it. The only real noise was coming from the rain outside and how it rattled at the windows. I felt positively tormented.

The room was deathly cold and I was suddenly worried I didn't have enough clothes with me and so I decided Marnie was right and returned the cornflakes and Coke to the kitchen, I would need at least another pair of jeans and some tops. I went back to my room.

"Where the fuck are you going?" whispers Marnie.

"I won't be a minute," I tell her and so I return to my room and fill my bag with more appropriate attire. I go back downstairs to where an irate Marnie awaits me.

"Are you with me or not?" she asks.

"Why, with you of course," I say.

Our escape was within our reach and as we crept closer to our dream it seemed impossible we would find it behind a closed door and down a lane, on a bus and then on a train. It just felt too easy and I was filled with trepidation.

Marnie

I reach quickly for the key hanging in the lock and frantically push at the door handle. It opens and we are free to leave, until I knock into Robert T. Macdonald, standing stiff across the threshold. He pushes me backward. I stumble to the floor. Nelly rushes to my side while he slams the door into its frame. The room shakes.

He drags me to my feet and shoves me onto a nearby chair. Nelly doesn't need to be pushed, she finds her own chair.

"You think I'm an idiot, don't you?" He is looking at me.

We shake our heads. We are afraid.

"You think I didn't know about this? About the money in the bag?"

I pale.

"I see you, Miss Marnie. I see you," he whispers.

"What about you, Nelly? You think I'm stupid?"

She shakes her head.

"Go up to your room," he instructs us. She doesn't want to.

"Get up to your fucking room!" he screams. She runs.

I am still and wait eagerly for a lecture, but he doesn't reach for a Bible, not this time, he reaches for the cuffs at the end of his sleeves and pulls them over his elbows. He cracks his knuckles and moves closer to the chair. He grabs me by the collar and then tautens his arm like an elastic band, ready to throw his fist into my face, and were it not for Mick standing behind him and pushing a gun into the back of his head that's exactly what he would have done.

Nelly

I sat at the top of the stairs and good golly it was the ice cream vendor and holding a gun of all things. Fortunately he went straight for Robert T. Macdonald and I have to say I was rather relieved.

"Help me with him," he says to Marnie. She was only too delighted.

"What do you want me to do?" Marnie asks.

"Tie him up with this." He throws her a rope.

It must have been very empowering tying Robert T. Macdonald up and with an ice cream vendor waving a gun in his face. She must have been thrilled to bits. I know I was. Marnie finds some masking tape. The captive was babbling all kinds of threats and warnings. It was imperative he be silenced. He might alert the ice cream vendor to my presence for example and that wouldn't do at all.

Once she was done the ice cream vendor became rather serious.

"Marnie," he says. "I'm only going to ask you this one more time. Where's my money?"

"I don't know. I told you."

He fired a bullet into the wall above her head. It was a confounded muddle.

"Gene and Izzy are dead!" she screamed. "They could have moved it anywhere." She really wanted that money and would die before handing it over to a cad selling ice cream and all kinds of confectionery. It was quite the pickle.

He points the gun at Robert T. Macdonald, who starts to whimper.

"Then how about I kill this guy," says Mick.

"I don't care," she says.

Robert T. Macdonald seemed pained. He starts to moan. Mick takes the gun and places it on his temple. He pulls on the trigger.

"Don't," says Marnie. "It's over there in the black tool bag."

Robert T. Macdonald blanked at her, he seemed confused, as I myself was. Why didn't she want him dead?

The ice cream vendor wandered over to the bag, all the while waving a gun at Marnie and Robert T. Macdonald.

The ice cream vendor opened the bag.

"My fucking money," he exclaimed. "How long have you had this bag, you little bitch?"

"Found it in the toolshed after you left," she says.

"Sure you did," he says.

He stopped waving the gun then and knelt to count his cash.

"It's all there." He smiled.

Marnie looked dejected while Robert T. Macdonald looked red and raging.

Mick sits next to Marnie.

"You know, Marnie, I didn't mean to be so hard on you back then."

He takes the gun and strokes her legs with it.

"What say you and me go upstairs and hang out for a while? Grandpa's not going anywhere. What do you think?"

Marnie smiles and follows him upstairs. I hide under the bed.

Marnie

I don't know what to do and so I give up the cash. I don't want to be around any more dead bodies and so I let Robert T. Macdonald live. Mick wants to fuck me and so I let him take me upstairs. I knew Nelly was there and hoped to God she wouldn't see. I hoped he'd take pity on us and give us a few pounds anyway, if only to get away from R. T. Macdonald.

I forget what it's like to be with Mick. He orders me to take off my clothes and starts taking off his own. He makes me lie on the bed. He thinks this is romantic. He tells me to spread my legs and kneels on the bottom of the bed. He flexes his muscles, he always flexed his muscles. He makes me think of Kirkland and I think I'm going to cry, but then Nelly shows up and smacks him on the head with a poker and he falls on top of me. I quickly crawl to the top of the bed.

"Gimme my clothes." She gathers them from the floor. I find an item of his clothing mixed up with mine and throw it away. I can't stop crying.

"Stop looking at me," I tell Nelly. She's seen me naked a thousand times but this was different. I felt ashamed.

She turns away and looks to Mick's body. He's still breathing. She gives him a kick in the stomach.

"For my sister," she spits.

"Thanks," I say.

"We'll lock him in here," she says, remembering Robert T. Macdonald has an outside lock on my door.

I grab for my money and we head downstairs.

Nelly

.

The ice cream vendor is quick to wake and is banging with a vengeance on Marnie's bedroom door. She tightens Robert T. Macdonald's rope and leaves the gun in the kitchen.

"I could have had Mick kill you but I didn't. Remember that about me."

She produces pictures. His pictures. Pictures of Izzy mostly.

"I'm taking a few of these with me. They're half mine anyway and I'll be keeping the wedding picture of you and my grandmother. You don't deserve to own it."

She shoves the pictures in her rucksack.

"I'm sure you have things to say but since I don't care what those things might be I guess you're going to have to listen to what I have to say. Lennie didn't murder Izzy and Gene. Izzy suffocated Gene with a cushion and then hanged herself in the shed. She committed suicide. It was Nelly and I who buried them in the garden, we didn't want to go into care and so we hid them. It had nothing to do with Lennie, not in the beginning. He found out what we did much later and when we weren't looking he moved their bodies under his rosebushes. He was trying to save us. You ever had a friend like that?"

She stands to leave.

"It's small consolation but if Izzy hadn't killed herself I

know she'd have welcomed you into her arms. She was weak like that."

When we have gathered all our belongings it is time to leave. It feels wrong to simply walk away.

"Toodle-oo, Gramps," I tell him and put a lead on the dog.

He moans behind the tape. He struggles with the rope, he tries to scream, but it is too late, the door is closed and we are on our way.

Marnie

It's a long journey to Firemore, especially with a dog, but when we get to the cottage we find Lennie's car in the driveway and a tall dark stranger we know to be Vlado.

How we welcomed the safety of his arms and how he welcomed the children of Lennie who wanted nothing more than to be held and cared for by the sea.

Later we slide rocks across the waters, bouncing them as far as we can throw. We eat fish and bread. We read books and watch a video about the queen of England. We sleep long and rise to sunshine and salt.

Over dinner I can see Vlado seeks a different kind of solace by the sea and the next morning I watch him race to the water until he is as far as a star and facing his own skies.

There is much to let go of in our hearts and, overwhelmed, Nelly and I also run to the water's edge and do not stop running until we have collected all of our griefs and secrets and sunk them far beneath the ocean. When I take my sister back to dry land we are wet and holding hands. Vlado brings us towels and laughter, so much laughter. I hope to know it always.

ACKNOWLEDGMENTS

So many people supported the writing of *The Death of Bees* and I will be forever grateful. Alex Christofi, my hardworking motivated agent at Conville and Walsh. The late John McGrath, who encouraged my voice and gave me confidence where there was none. Writer Sergio Casci, who read the first screenplay I ever wrote, placing me on a path that changed my life. Moonstone International 1999, where I was mentored by the finest of writers. The team at William Heinemann for their faith and enthusiasm. Michael Signorelli for his zealous commitment. Everyone at HarperCollins for their efficiency and support.

ABOUT THE AUTHOR

Lisa O'Donnell won the Orange Screenwriting Prize in 2000 for *The Wedding Gift* and, in the same year, was nominated for the Dennis Potter New Screenwriters Award. A native of Scotland, she is now a full-time writer and lives in Los Angeles with her two children. *The Death of Bees* is her first novel.